P9-COO-378

THESE DARN HEELS

THESE DARN HEELS

•

Julie Stone

AVALON BOOKS
NEW YORK

Published by Thomas Bouregy & Co., Inc.
160 Madison Avenue, New York, NY 10016

Library of Congress Cataloging-in-Publication Data

Stone, Julie.
These darn heels / Julie Stone.
p. cm.
ISBN 0-8034-9772-5 (hardcover : alk. paper)
1. Young women—Fiction. 2. Greeting cards industry—Fiction.
3. Dating (Social customs)—Fiction. 4. Chicago (Ill.)—Fiction.
I. Title.
PS3619.T6568T44 2006
813'.6—dc22
2005035234

PRINTED IN THE UNITED STATES OF AMERICA
ON ACID-FREE PAPER
BY HADDON CRAFTSMEN, BLOOMSBURG, PENNSYLVANIA

For Jake and Brett, who show me everyday,
what is important. And to Chad, your love
and support make my world go round.

Chapter One

Alex Sanders took in the beautiful ballroom. The dim lights cast a soft glow and the air hummed with the murmur of polite conversation. Raised to attend glittering events like this, Alex spent her entire adult life avoiding them. But here she was nevertheless and, if she didn't mind saying so, she looked pretty darn good.

Pausing at the top of the stairs, she surveyed the crowd below her, trying to spy her friend and cohort for the evening, Claire. Unlike Alex, she actually seemed excited about being there.

"I can't believe your father has tickets to The Chicago Art Guild Gala. The *Tribune* called it *the* event of the season," she had gushed in the car on the way over.

"Yeah, lucky us," Alex had replied through tight lips. It still steamed her that even though she was twenty-six, her parents could command her presence at one of their society events just so they could parade her around in front of their friends.

But here she was in all her socially acceptable glory—

1

black cocktail dress and heels that were the perfect height, though she wobbled in them. Her hair pulled up as best it could be, with just a few stubborn wisps escaping in a way she thought was attractive. Her eyes accented with a hint of brown shadow and her lips glossed with a natural sheen.

"Alexandria," a voice purred from her left. Alex bristled as she turned to see a woman she recognized from either her mother's bridge club or charity guild. She couldn't be certain, because they all blended together in a collage of floral skirts, high-pitched voices and wine spritzers from her childhood. All were perfect clones of her mother, but with a variety of hair colors.

"How wonderful that you've come," the woman continued, her voice as sugary as artificial sweetener. "Your mother tells me your new little hobby is taking up a great deal of your time."

Alex almost stretched her arms behind her to pull the knife out of her back that her mother continually stuck there when it came to her shop.

"Hobby is an interesting way of describing it," she replied. She might have to come to this thing, but she didn't have to be insulted by anyone.

"Really, what would you call it then? It's some sort of boutique or something, right?"

The look of confusion on the woman's face seemed so genuine Alex felt it was her duty to set her straight. She sweetened her tone to speak her language.

"Well, it's not really a boutique. It's a card shop, but it's so much more than that." Alex couldn't help but smile as she talked about her little store. "I like to think of it as a philosophy of communication."

"It sounds lovely. I'll have to find my way to you the

next time I need a birthday card. By the way, you look exquisite as usual. The single men will be lining up to talk to you later. Now *that* would give your dear mother something to talk about."

And with that she pecked Alex on the cheek and turned to continue through the party circuit before Alex could reply.

That last comment didn't surprise her much. It was, after all, her mother's goal in life to marry her off.

Alex had no time for romance. She poured all her time and energy into her shop, an oasis for people who wanted to reach out to one another. But cards alone couldn't keep the shop afloat, so she also designed invitations for parties, birth announcements, and the dreaded wedding invitations.

Snapping her mind back to the party, Alex adjusted her dress and resumed her search for Claire. Finally, she spied her across the room by the bar, deep in conversation with Alex's father. Alex shuddered with annoyance.

"Better just say hello and get it over with," she muttered to herself, and then stepped off, relieved that at least her mother had yet to make an appearance. That relief didn't last long as she realized her foot hadn't caught the step.

Arms flailing, Alex searched desperately for anything that would stop her fall. Unfortunately, what she caught was the arm of a waiter balancing a full tray of shrimp. Instead of keeping her from falling, he joined in and the two of them soon found themselves at the bottom of the grand staircase covered in shrimp, lemon, and whatever fancy lettuce had been used as a garnish.

Luckily, the cocktail sauce had missed her completely, but the waiter hadn't fared as well. The poor guy looked so confused she just had to laugh, until she realized that no one else seemed to find it amusing. They all looked horrified in the way that only socialites can, and suddenly Alex was just as mortified.

"I am so sorry," she said to him as they both scrambled to their feet, her cheeks burning and probably the color of the cocktail sauce on his arm.

Finally upright, Alex smiled apologetically, anxious to move out of the spotlight. But as she stepped down on her right foot, it was apparent that more than her pride was hurt.

Pain shot through her ankle and her whole leg seemed to give in. Just as she thought she was going to give a repeat performance, she felt a hand on her arm grab hold to steady her.

"Thank goodness," she said as she spun on her good foot, but it wasn't Claire's familiar face that greeted her. Instead, she found herself in the arms of a man she had never seen before, and the amused smile on his face did little to improve her mood.

"No problem," he said, obviously trying to stifle the offending grin.

Alex's blood pressure rose. Her eyebrows arched and she opened her mouth to let him have it, but before she could utter a word, Claire was by her side.

"Alex, are you all right?" She asked, and Alex quickly realized Claire had saved her from what could have been her second embarrassing scene of the night.

It just figured this would happen to her here. Her parents had insisted she come. And parents or not, it was the only social invitation she had accepted in months, not that she didn't get her fair share of offers.

But by divine intervention, Claire had stepped in and saved her from offering up her opinion to the smiling stranger. Putting her arm around Alex's waist, Claire helped her hobble away.

"Nice move," she whispered as they made their way awkwardly up the stairs, Alex leaning most of her weight on her and trying to balance the other side with the handrail.

"Please tell me my father didn't see that," she said through her forced smile.

"He was educating the bartender on the aging of scotch or something, so you're in the clear if we can get you out of here quickly," Claire said with urgency in her voice. There was nothing she loved more then a little drama.

They continued their pace to the coat check, where Alex let go of Claire just long enough to slip her black wool coat around her shoulders and wrap her coordinating scarf around her neck. Then they scurried out the door as best they could.

"I'll wait here while you get the car," Alex announced as she plopped herself down on the bench in front of the hotel. She bent down, slipped her strappy black shoe from her foot, and began rubbing at her sore ankle. As if that would really make it feel any better.

"These darn heels," she muttered to herself. No matter how great they looked, she should have known better than to try to wear them. When it came to balance and grace, Alex was sorely lacking.

"You should put some snow on that ankle; it'll help keep the swelling down."

Alex jumped at the male voice and turned to see a familiar smile. The tiny black cocktail bag she called a purse was in his hand. Embarrassment flooded her cheeks once again.

Snow? Was he insane? There wasn't a chance in hell she was going to put snow on her ankle and add to the spectacle.

"Thank you for that helpful hint, but I think it can wait until I get home," she said flatly. Why was he still smiling at her?

"Well, depending on traffic and where you live it could be awhile. Snow can only help," he said, sitting down beside her.

"What are you, some kind of survival expert?" Her voice picked up speed as she went on. "You might have noticed we're in the heart of downtown Chicago. If I need medical attention, I could probably do better than some dirty snow off the sidewalk."

"Hostile, I see. Embarrassed, perhaps? You know, you really shouldn't be. For the price of those tickets, there should have been some sort of entertainment. The way I see it, you did that stuffy place a favor, and to answer your rhetorical question, no."

He smiled at her, a nice smile, an almost perfect smile with straight, white teeth.

"No? No, what?" The pain in her ankle was starting to affect her brain or something, because she had no idea what he was talking about, though she thought she probably should.

They were interrupted by the honking of a car horn as Claire pulled directly in front of them, splashing slush and water onto Alex's bare foot and the offending black shoe that was still squeezed onto her right foot.

"Hey, can you help me get her in the car?" She asked brightly, and before Alex could open her mouth to object, the guy had his arm around her waist and the two of them were maneuvering her toward the car. They paused only to open the door, and then they eased her into the passenger seat.

"Good luck with that," he said, pointing to her foot and then handed her the tiny purse before closing the door.

Then he turned and started talking to Claire, but to her dismay, Alex couldn't hear a word they were saying because Claire had the heater in the car turned on full blast. Not that it was doing anything to warm it up.

Ice cold air blew at her from every direction and by the time she found the dial to turn it down, Claire was climbing into the driver side.

"What'd he say? What were you two talking about out there?" Her ankle felt like it was on fire.

"Whoa! Slow down there, Grace. He was just telling me where I should take you to get your ankle looked at."

"So, is he a doctor or just a know-it-all? Do you know that he actually wanted me to put snow on my ankle? And stop calling me Grace, I can't help it that I'm clumsy!" she said incredulously.

"A doctor, actually, and the snow is not a bad idea. It probably would have numbed the pain and helped keep the swelling down. So, where do you want to go, emergency room or urgent care?"

"I turned my ankle. It's no big deal. At this point, I just want to go home and get out of this dress, not to mention the hose, slip, and shoes. Then curl up with my standard Saturday night dates, Ben and Jerry. But maybe you and Dr. Perfect Teeth could meet up at the Urgent Care and have a good laugh over me and my ankle."

She knew she was being ridiculous, but something about the well-intentioned stranger just got to her.

Helpful or not, handsome or not, Alex just wanted this evening to be over. She rubbed the ankle to make her point, but all that rubbing really wasn't doing it any good.

Claire shook her head, stifling a laugh. Alex glared at her from the passenger seat, then leaned over and turned the heater back up, now that it was actually blowing warm air.

The sudden gust of air blew her already unruly hair into her eyes, and when she reached up to pat it back into place, her hand touched something cold and slimy. She gave it a yank and was appalled to find it was a piece of shrimp.

One look at it and she erupted into giggles, waving it in Claire's direction. She burst out laughing, too, eventually so hard that she could no longer drive and had to pull into another loading zone and stop the car.

"If you could have seen yourself—one minute the picture of composure, in control of the room, the next lying in a heap at the bottom of the stairs covered in appetizers." Claire held her sides, gasping for air.

"This is what I get for listening to you. 'Just go to the gala for your parents. What harm could it do? Maybe we can even drum up some business.'" Alex rolled her eyes. "I should have known better. Society and I do not mix, no matter what my last name is."

She handed Claire her scarf. "Now, will you please get out and fill this with snow, my ankle is killing me."

Claire looked at her with fake shock and then obliged, piling snow from the sidewalk into the black scarf. In the car she handed it back, and Alex laid it onto her sore ankle.

"How long till it feels better, did the good doctor say?"

"Nope. Mostly he wanted me to know where I should

take you to have it X-rayed." Claire shot her a knowing
look. "But he must be a pretty good judge of people."

"Now why would you say that?" Alex asked, lifting
the snow to have another look at her swelling ankle.

"Because he told me that when you refused to go, I
should at least make sure you could wiggle your toes,"
Claire answered, putting the car into drive and pulling out.

Alex turned on the light, set her foot on the dash-
board, and wiggled her newly pedicured toes in the dim
light. They had popped through her panty hose during
the fall and the sight of them made her giggle again, but
she managed to control herself.

"Did you check to make sure this snow wasn't yellow?"

"With all that frozen gray slush, who could tell? I'm
sure it's fine."

She put it back on her ankle and held the dripping
scarf there until Claire pulled up in front of her apartment. Somehow, the two of them managed to get her out
of the car and up the slippery sidewalk to the front door.

Inside, Alex hopped into the living room and fell
onto the couch, where she was immediately greeted by
Milo, her cocker spaniel, jumping up beside her and
licking her cheek.

"You're not going to stay and just look at me all
night, are you?" she asked as Claire handed her the ice
bag she had made in the kitchen. "You're all dressed
up. Go back to the party, head to the bars, something. I
have your cell-phone number in case, I don't know, my
toes stop wiggling or whatever." She waved her hands
toward the door, hoping Claire would take the not-so-
subtle hint and take off.

"Well, I do spiff up pretty well, and it is the social event of the season," she said, jumping up from her chair. "Seriously, if you need anything, do call. If I don't hear from you, I will see you Monday morning with coffee in hand; maybe even one of those scones you like so much."

"You must either feel really bad about leaving or really sorry about talking me into going in the first place," Alex said, her guilt over ruining her friend's evening subsiding.

"Neither. It'll be more like a celebration," Claire replied as she smiled mischievously at her.

"And why is that?" Alex wondered where in the world Claire was going with this.

Claire backed toward the door. "I told 'Dr. Perfect Teeth'—as you called him—where he could find you on Monday. He said he wanted to check on you."

Alex stared at her blankly, not knowing what to say.

Why in the world would that doctor want to check on her, especially when she'd been so horrible to him?

Alex started to object, but Claire was already out the door, yelling good-bye over her shoulder.

"Coward!" She yelled.

Setting her ice aside, she hopped into her bedroom and pulled off her dress. She held it to her nose.

"Shrimp. It's the dry cleaner for you," she said, wadding up the soft fabric and throwing it on the chair.

Milo sighed from his bed in the corner. Pulling on her favorite flannel pajama bottoms and an old sweatshirt, Alex hopped into the kitchen, got the ice cream out of the freezer, tossed the lid, and grabbed a spoon. When she finally reached the couch, she looked at her ankle. It had already doubled in size and glistened in shades of purple and red. Shaking her head, she put the ice back onto it.

Picking up the remote, she mindlessly flipped the channels looking for anything of interest, maybe an old episode of 90210 or something. She paused when she came to a commercial for toothpaste. It flashed picture after picture of smiling people with perfect teeth, just like the good doctor had.

There was just something about him. She couldn't put her finger on it, but it intrigued her. Maybe it was just the smile—she'd never seen anyone with teeth so straight and white.

It went against her nature, but she felt a flutter of excitement that he had asked where to find her.

But soon the cynical voice in her head took over. He may have asked, *but would he follow through?*

Chapter Two

"Earth to Peter, come in Peter."

Dr. Peter Gibson gave an annoyed look across the table.

"Very funny, Michael," he replied to the man who sat with him in the doctors' lounge. The two of them were wrapping up their shift in the Emergency Room by updating the charts of the patients they had seen that day. It was mindless work compared to the exhausting day they had both put in as residents, and Peter welcomed the chance to just let his mind wander for a minute.

It immediately focused on the woman he had encountered at the Art Gala on Saturday night. Truth be told, it had whenever he had found a minute of free time in the last forty-eight hours.

"Man, where were you?" Michael asked, clicking the pen in his hand repeatedly.

For a split second, Peter considered telling Michael all about the woman who had occupied his free moments—

how her first reaction to causing a scene had been to laugh at herself. Or maybe he could tell him how just one ringlet had escaped its clip and had curled so delicately to the nape of her neck—what harm could it do?

"Just thinking about my weekend," he answered coolly, embarrassed that a woman whose name he didn't even know could have this effect on him, like he was some hormone-charged teenager.

"Oh, right, the Arts Gala or whatever it was. Did you make any good contacts?"

That was Michael, always working a room, looking for anyone who would give him a boost in his career. Peter, on the other hand, relied on hard work and hours of studying to succeed.

They were very different, the two of them, but both good doctors. For Peter, the fast-paced environment of the ER had felt like home from the minute their rotation started, but for Michael it was overwhelming. He preferred the plotted out slowness of their last rotation—surgery. Their differences had served them well since med school. And though they were competitive, they were also friends.

"No, I didn't meet any 'contacts'. But—" Peter hesitated.

Michael smiled. "But what? Man, you and I have been together for the last eighteen hours and your head has been somewhere else the entire time. So, whatever is keeping your head out of the game, tell me."

"There was a woman there. She fell, and I helped her up and we talked for a minute and I cannot quit thinking about her." Peter felt foolish saying even that much.

"Jeez, Peter. A woman, you can't be serious. You have it made, here. Dating the chief of staff's daughter, meeting all the right people—your future is set. And here you are mooning over some klutz you met at a party. Get over it, or give me a crack at Ashleigh Rogers. I could get used to being the favored future son-in-law." Michael shook his head in disbelief.

"Shift's over, I'm going to get some shut-eye," he continued, standing and gathering up the clipboards on the table in front of him. "Get your head together; we're back on at six A.M." And then he was gone, leaving Peter alone in the lounge.

Peter could feel his cheeks flood with embarrassment. He should have known better then to tell Michael. He couldn't possibly understand that Peter didn't want to be the favored future son-in-law. Ashleigh was a great girl, but it had been obvious to him from the start that they were different, too different. The problem was that she was so focused on marrying a doctor, it didn't seem to matter who he was.

And now, after a brief encounter with a woman he'd never met, he felt like his whole body was buzzing. He had to see her again, if for no other reason than to get his focus back. He couldn't afford to be so distracted. Though he had a sneaking suspicion seeing her again was only going to make matters worse.

The shop was a madhouse on Monday. Alex was so busy she barely noticed the pain in her ankle or her limp as she made her way from one customer to the next. Thankfully, she'd had yesterday to stay off of it because she barely sat down all day.

It was good to be so busy; the weeks before Valentine's Day always were. She had stocked up for the holiday and was running her usual "make your own Valentine" promotion.

The table she usually used to consult with future brides was piled high with construction paper, scissors and other bits and pieces to make something special for the one you love. All that mess was really enough to make her physically ill, but she had to ignore it. It was something unique to her store and she to put up with it. After all, if people wanted to send the same old cards, a Hallmark store could be found at practically every corner.

When she finally did sit down, it was to work on party invitations that had been ordered earlier in the day. This was the part of her job she loved: taking her ideas and matching them with what the customer needed.

She knew she was just delaying what she had to do that night: dinner with her father. But since he, or his money rather, had funded the opening of Correspondence, she had to make time for him when he requested.

He made her nervous, always questioning her ability to run her own store, even though his accountants did her books and she had always shown a profit. At least her mother wasn't with him. It was hard enough to field the professional questions without dodging the ones about her love life at the same time.

Growing up with her parents had been interesting. Their marriage was hardly a model of domestic bliss. Constant attempts to mold the other into someone he or she wasn't, followed by periods of indifference and silence. Throw in the pressure of life in the highest tax bracket and you have one messed up household.

Alex knew all of this probably added to her commit-

ment phobia, but the energy it would take to figure it all
out just never seemed worth it. She was particularly
happy with her current life—she had the shop, her
friends, and her dog. An occasional date and some
innocent flirting were all she was really interested in,
anyway.

Checking her watch, she was annoyed to see it was
almost six. Dinner with Dad was to begin at seven, and
with her new limp, it would take a bit longer than usual
to get over to the restaurant.

There wouldn't be time to print the cards out tonight—
maybe she'd come in early tomorrow. She needed to or-
ganize the chaos Valentine's season was causing, anyway.

Just as she stepped into the back room and flipped
off the music, the bells on the front door jingled. With
a groan, she glanced at the door.

It was probably Claire; she hadn't been in with coffee this morning as she had promised, and after desert-
ing her Saturday night, too. Maybe Alex could guilt her
into driving her to dinner with her dad. Or better yet,
make Claire join them at dinner and take some of the
pressure off.

She emerged from the curtain ready to lay it on
thick. "Sure, first it's no coffee this morning, and now
showing up at the end of the day . . ." Her voice trailed
off as she realized it was not Claire, but Dr. Perfect
Teeth. "Oh, hi," she said weakly.

"I didn't know I was supposed to bring you coffee. I
was too busy ducking your words to listen to them. I
see from your lack of crutches you weren't listening to
mine, either," he quipped, a broad smile on his face.

Even with the great teeth, who smiles this much?

Alex wondered, although even her sarcastic inner voice couldn't stop a shiver from running down her arms.

"No, no hospital. No crutches, toes are still wiggling, so thanks for checking in on me, but I don't think I have insurance for house calls."

She hobbled toward him, doing her best to walk as normally as possible, but not doing a very good job. It seemed like defeat to show her injury. Finally, she reached her desk and leaned against it in her best nonchalant manner.

But he wasn't buying it. The smile gone, he suddenly looked very serious. His eyes traveled down her body, finally stopping at her feet. It wasn't exactly how she wanted to be checked out.

Then he knelt down in front of her. She glanced from him to the window at the front of her shop. Anyone passing by would think he was proposing or something.

"What are you doing?" she said, looking down at him, flustered by the position. "I told you I was fine."

"Yes, I can see how fine you are," he said seriously. "Now listen, whether you like it or not, I *am* going to take a look at that ankle. I took an oath to care for those in need, and it's obvious you're in need. So sit back on that desk and let me look. I won't even send you a bill."

His eyes sparkled a bit as he said it. Dark blue eyes, with long black lashes.

Since he was already pulling off her shoe, she had no choice but to agree. And at this point, her ankle was really throbbing, and having it looked at was starting to seem like a good idea. So she slid back onto the desk, knocking over her pen cup, and pushing the keyboard onto the floor.

"Seriously, I'd like to say I'm not usually so accident-prone, but that would be a lie. I've always been clumsy, but typically, I don't really hurt myself. Just surface wounds." She giggled a little bit.

Who was this person talking and giggling? Had she gone completely mental in the last few minutes?

He peeled her sock off and then held her foot. Gently he turned it this way and that, his hands warm and soft. A tremor went through her. How could anyone except a newborn baby have such soft skin?

"Does that hurt?" he asked, looking up at her intently, his fingers pressing into the part of her ankle that was the most technicolor. The pain roared up her leg and she kicked him in response. He fell backward into a rack of cards.

Mortified, Alex jumped up to help, forgetting somehow about the shooting pain in her leg.

This was a big mistake and the undoing of the entire situation. She stepped down onto her left foot, and whether it was the actual injury, or the twisting and prodding, it gave out completely and she fell, landing directly on top of him.

Alex was appalled; why did she keep falling? And this time on top of this very handsome doctor.

Their faces were inches apart, and she could smell his breath, warm and sweet on her face. Not a surprise, really, that his breath would be perfect, too. She felt her pulse quicken.

Amazingly, he was still smiling, but not as broadly. Probably the shock of what had just happened to him had left him stunned. She was just about to make some remark that would make light of the situation when the bells on the door rang out.

She turned—rolled really—to see who in the world was coming in to buy a card at this hour. She was closed, for Pete's sake! An older man walked toward them, peering down with disapproval.

Alex gasped.

"Dad! What are you doing here?"

Chapter Three

Certainly this was one of those situations that couldn't possibly get any worse—how could it? Awkwardly, Alex got to her feet. Doctor Perfect Teeth scrambled up beside her once she was off him. Her father stood feet away from them, shaking his head.

"I thought I would stop by and offer you a ride to dinner," he said somewhat disdainfully. "Really Alexandria, the door to the store was open. Anyone could have come and seen you rolling around the floor with . . ." He looked at her, obviously waiting for an introduction to the man standing beside her.

Alex stammered. "Um, ah . . ."

She couldn't make the introduction because she didn't know Dr. Perfect Teeth's name herself. The blood that had built up in her swollen ankle surged to her cheeks. Feeling like a sixteen-year-old girl who had just been discovered on the couch necking with some boy, she wondered how in the world she was going to explain this to her father.

"Peter Gibson, sir." The words seemed to ring out, a little loud in Alex's opinion. At least this solved her first problem. Now she knew his name. He held his hand out toward Mr. Sanders, but put it back into his pocket when it was ignored.

"Mr. Gibson," her father started condescendingly, but Alex cut him off.

"*Doctor* Gibson, actually, Dad." Why in the world this would make it any better she didn't know, but his being a doctor suddenly felt like a detail that shouldn't just be swept under the carpet.

The expression on her father's face didn't change. And Alex swelled with annoyance as she suddenly remembered she was not, in fact sixteen, and she hadn't been necking with anyone. Though she very well could have been if her father had waited just two minutes longer to make his grand entrance, but that was completely beside the point.

"Doctor? Well, that will make your mother happy. Too bad she wasn't the one to walk in on this scene."

His dismissive tone reminded Alex of herself the other night when Dr. Gibson had tried to help her on the park bench, and it was obvious she had inherited her father's crass way with strangers.

It was not an attractive quality.

"Dad, really! Peter, um, Dr. Gibson, I mean," she stammered, limping to her desk, collecting herself a bit. "I twisted my ankle the other night." As she spoke, she said a silent prayer that her father didn't realize she had fallen at the gala. But there was no stopping now.

"Dr. Gibson was there, and he was kind enough to check on me today. I fell again when he was looking at my ankle, and that's when you came in."

Her eyes went from her father's hard stare to Peter's bemused grin, and she felt the heat return to her face. That smile, his eyes, those lashes. Boy, when you put the pieces together, he was really quite attractive.

"So, what's the diagnosis, Doctor?" she asked, trying to be all business and ignore her father's huffing next to her.

"Well, I'm fairly certain nothing is broken, but you need to stay off that foot for a while. I think it's safe to say that every time you move, you run the risk of further injury." His voice, so very serious and official-sounding, almost caused Alex to burst out laughing.

He continued, "Normally, I would suggest crutches, but I'm not sure—given your balance challenges—that would be such a good idea. I think if you can try to take it easy for a few days, you'll be good as new." He walked toward the desk where she sat, and pulled some sort of bandage out of his pocket.

"You should wrap it to keep it immobile. I brought you this, and here's my card if you should have any other questions." Laying it on the desk, he turned and walked toward the door, pausing in front of her father, who stood silently observing.

"Mr. Sanders, I apologize that our introduction was under such awkward circumstances. I hope you enjoy dinner with your daughter. I'm sure that I would." Then he continued out the door, leaving both of the Sanderses speechless, though for completely different reasons.

Alex turned her gaze away from the closing door and faced her father. It was perhaps the first time she had seen him speechless. She rose as quickly as she could, and limped over to pick up her coat and purse, which had fallen to the floor.

"So, you're here to give me a ride?" She hoped she could change the subject and move their dinner along. This was not the start she had wanted for this evening.

Sales, though by no means bad, had been down in the last quarter. The holidays had not proved to be very merry. He must have gotten the figures by now, and she knew another lecture about her business decisions was on the agenda.

They had vastly different ideas about the direction the store should go. When she had approached him about backing the shop, it had been for a few reasons. Obviously, the first had been that she had a dream to open this quaint, very personal place where people could go to find a way to express their feelings, and she had no money.

The other had been to try to reach out to her father on his level. They hadn't been close in years, and this was a way to find some common ground. Or so Alex had hoped.

It hadn't worked as she thought it would. She wanted everything to be unique and personal. Her dad wanted it to be a financial blockbuster. No matter how successful it was, it was never going to be what he pictured. Actually, it was the exact opposite. So these little dinner meetings were never fun.

He offered her his arm without a word and helped her out to the car. They drove through the city traffic, making small talk about her mother and his business meetings. Not a word was spoken about the good doctor.

When they reached the restaurant and the valet

opened the door, she gave him a little smile with her thank-you. Flirting was actually something she was good at when she tried.

Her father came around and offered her his arm. He escorted her into the restaurant, barely pausing at the maitre'd stand before continuing to his usual table.

When they had ordered their drinks—a martini for her, and a scotch on the rocks for him—he smiled at her.

"You know, I think I should ask for my money back from all those dance classes you took. Did you think about having a real doctor take a look at you?" The ice clinked in his glass as he took a sip from his drink, looking beyond her at the people in the crowded restaurant.

"Aside from the spectacle I caused, there really isn't that much damage done. I was just on my feet too much today. Things were really busy at the store." Her mouth was dry so she took a long drink from her martini. Humor from her dad was unusual—she suspected something was up.

He sighed and looked at his menu, apparently distracted from commenting by the sudden appearance of the waiter, who listed the specials.

Alex listened intently to the waiter, her mind spinning at what had come over her father. Jokes, sighing, small talk—something was definitely going on. They ordered their food and another scotch for him. Finally, he cleared his throat and looked across the table at her.

Fearing another overblown lecture, she rushed on, "Listen, Dad, I know that it was a little crazy when you got to the store, but I told you exactly what happened, so if you're mad about it or something, why don't we just lay it out on the table so that we can get on with it."

This was excruciating. It was like the time she drove the car through the garage, and he made her sit with him while he met with the insurance adjuster.

"Alex, to be honest, if what I saw at the store had been what I thought it was, this whole dinner would be different."

This was a curve ball if she'd ever seen one. What in the world could that possibly mean? The look on her face must have translated exactly what she was thinking, because he barely paused as he continued.

"Your mother is very concerned about your social life. Or lack thereof, I should say. She wants me to stop helping you with the shop so that you can spend more of your time 'socially,' as she put it. I'm afraid I'm not going to be able to rent you that space after all." His voice sped up as he came to the end of the sentence, trailing off behind the glass of scotch that he quickly raised to his lips and drank dry. Magically, as he set it down the waiter appeared with a fresh one.

Alex couldn't speak, she was so stunned. She felt like checking herself in the mirror just to make sure she hadn't been transported back to the eighteenth century. Insanity, that's what it was. Her mother had lost her mind; her father, too, for that matter. They should talk about *that,* not about closing the store. What could her mother possibly be thinking?

"So, just so I'm clear on this," Alex began slowly. "The deal we had—that you would rent me space in your new retail development—is off. And Mother thinks that since my lease is up and, without you, Correspondence will have nowhere to go, I will just close it down and join her for cards and drinks at the club, meet a suitable husband and get married?"

She was screeching by the time she finished. The older couple at the table next to them turned to look in her direction. As her father motioned for her to keep her voice down, she felt herself teetering on the brink of becoming ballistic.

"I know, it's crazy, but she is adamant about it. And from a fiscal standpoint, you haven't shown a significant return on investment. While you aren't losing money, you aren't growing as much as you should be, according to my accountant. Maybe it *is* time to move on." His voice changed back to the familiar straight-talking businessman she was used to. This angle she could handle.

"Listen, Dad, I never wanted to corner the market on greeting cards. I had a philosophy about people communicating with each other; that's why I opened the store. I know that we are only showing a modest profit, and that's fine with me. You and I have this discussion every quarter, and we are never going to agree. But this thing with Mom, it's insanity, you have to see that." She couldn't believe she was even having this conversation. She banged her sore ankle against her chair leg just to make sure this wasn't some twisted nightmare.

"Insanity? Yes, I do see that, but from her perspective, you can't be happy with your life. All her friends' children are getting engaged, planning weddings, going to parties. All she has to show are the invitations you printed for her bridge luncheon. I am not agreeing with her, but I'm also tired of hearing about it. The only way to get around this is for you to convince her she is wrong."

He said this as if it were possible. Her mother was never wrong.

"Or I could negotiate a new lease with my landlord," she said, suddenly defiant. However, her bravado was in word only. Her father had negotiated her original lease, and he knew the market. That low-rent lease was up and the landlord was looking for more money; that was why she had planned to move the shop in the first place.

Her father looked at her and sighed greatly. "Alex, we both know a comparable lease isn't likely. Please, just talk to your mother."

Alex knew he was right, as infuriating as it was. Her father had a way of seeing just the business side of things, leaving the emotion out of it. Her mother had obviously put her foot down.

"You think that if I can convince her that the store, my life, is a normal version of success—which, by the way, it is—then she'll get off your back and we can go back to our original deal, moving Correspondence?"

Okay, that was at least a plan. She could have lunch at the club, show her mother how happy she was, show her some of the promotions she planned for the spring, and maybe even get her to bring her friends in for their invitation needs. As she thought it through, it seemed almost sensible. The first sensible thing that had happened since her father stepped into the store that night.

"No, I'm telling you that you need to convince her you do have a successful social life. That doctor would be the answer to her prayers." He looked her directly in the eye. "Why don't you tell me more about him?"

That's when Alex knew she was in serious trouble.

Chapter Four

As the door shut behind him, Peter shook his head in disbelief at what he had just done. What had come over him to toss that remark out about enjoying dinner with Alex? Alex—or rather, Alexandria—as her father had called her when he walked in on them. *What would he have found if he had appeared a few seconds later?* Peter wondered.

He turned and walked up the street and away from her shop. The snow crunched under his feet, and though the air around him was frigid, he barely felt the chill. An elevated train rattled by above him, the one he should have been on, but he was tired of always doing what he "should". Maybe that was why he'd come up here in the first place.

Across the street, a neon beer sign glowed in the window of a local tavern. For once, he wasn't on call, and he'd already missed his train. One drink and he'd be on his way, hopefully with his head a little bit clearer.

Inside the dim, smoke-filled room, he found a seat at

the bar and took off his coat. The bartender, a man about his age in a worn flannel shirt, set a napkin in front of him.

"What'll you have?" he asked.

"Whatever you have on draft is fine." And with that said, Peter pulled out his wallet and handed the bartender a ten-dollar bill.

"So, what do you do?" The bartender wiped a wet spot from the bar with a towel, and then slung it over his shoulder.

"I'm a doctor, or will be. I'm finishing up my second year of residency at Mercy Hospital."

"Whew," he whistled, rubbing his fingers together, making the Universal sign for money.

"Actually, that's not why I got into medicine."

A man appeared at the other end of the bar and waved an empty mug in their direction.

"Hold on, duty calls, but I gotta hear the rest of this." The bartender turned and went to get the man his refill.

Peter could hardly wait. The reaction he got when he told people that he wanted to be a doctor to help people was generally the same—a look of disbelief combined with a sarcastic "yeah, right."

Peter—the small town boy who had paid for college and med school with a combination of student loans and part-time jobs—didn't want his future handed to him; he wanted to earn it.

And if he were going to have a heart to heart with the bartender, he would prefer it be about Alex. What was it about her that had caused him to take the El up here?

He tried to tell himself that it was merely concern about her ankle, but he had trouble lying to himself.

He'd been drawn to her even before she fell. Actually,

she'd first caught his eye at the buffet, and not just because she was gorgeous. No, it was how she acted; wiggling in her dress, as if it was uncomfortable. The way she chose the cheese and crackers and the raw vegetables, leaving behind the caviar and the smoked salmon puffs. She seemed, like him, to be out of place. Something about her called out to him that she was a kindred spirit.

Then she had taken that spectacular fall and laughed about it. She was more than just a pretty face, that's what it was. Classy, but clumsy, he thought.

"So?" The bartender returned, interrupting Peter's train of thought.

"To help people," he answered, almost defiantly.

"That's cool. You don't meet too many people like that, at least I don't." He seemed genuinely impressed. "I suppose you make house calls, too." He laughed and Peter chuckled.

"Actually, I took the El up here to check in on this girl, though I'm pretty sure it had nothing to do with her health."

"Now this sounds like a good story." He picked up Peter's mug, and Peter was surprised to see it was empty. "You want another beer before you tell me that one?"

"Want, yes. But lately what I want isn't important. I'll take a glass of water, though."

The bartender nodded, filled another glass with water, and set it down on the same damp napkin.

"Just so you know, I realize how pathetic I sound about all this. People have bigger problems. It's just that I've always had a plan for my life, and I've gotten off track somehow." He took a long drink of his water.

"How do you mean?"

The girl I met; we were at this Art Gala, and she acted just as uncomfortable as I felt. It reminded me of myself, I guess."

"Hey, bartender, we need some drinks down here."

Peter turned to see a group of beautiful young women at the end of the bar who must have just come in from the cold.

"Seeing something of yourself in another person is a good thing. Take it from me—I know more about people then any shrink."

And just like that, he was on to his next customer, shrugging at Peter as he walked backward toward the gaggle of girls.

As if on cue, the cell phone in his pocket rang. He pulled it out and checked the number on the display: Ashleigh. He switched it off so the call would go to his voicemail.

He stood and pulled on his coat, leaving the change from his beer next to the damp napkin.

"Hey, thanks," his new friend behind the bar called out as Peter made his way to the door, and he turned and waved.

In his life, Peter had relied on many generous people, and he tried to return the favor when he could—karma, or whatever you wanted to call it. Besides, the guy was a great listener.

The cold air filled his lungs as he stepped outside and started back toward the train stop. At least the beer had relaxed him somewhat. He pulled his phone out of his pocket and turned it on. No need to check the messages—he knew what they would say. Ironically, as he went to put it back in his pocket, its shrill ring cut through the quiet night. He couldn't hide forever.

"Hello."

"Where the hell are you?" A familiar voice screeched into his ear.

"Ashleigh, calm down. I got held up," he said, stretching the truth a bit. "I'm sorry. Just sit tight. I'm on my way."

"Fine, just hurry, okay?"

His apology worked to some extent—at least she stopped screeching—but the new, sweet tone she took on grated his nerves almost as much.

"This dinner with Daddy is very important for our—" she caught herself, "*Your* future."

"Yes, I know." And just like that, his tension returned. "You told me. I have to hurry if I'm going to get the next train. See you soon. Good-bye."

"Try to think of something medical you did today that will impress Daddy on your way," she added coyly. "Bye, honey!" And then she hung up.

"Medical. Well, honey, I took the train up to Lincoln Park to examine the ankle of the most intriguing woman," he muttered to himself as he snapped his phone shut. That would be impressive, though "daddy" probably wouldn't think so, and Ashleigh would think even less of it. But then again, she had a hard time thinking of anything more than the diamond rings in the window of Tiffany's lately.

Peter had met Ashleigh at a reception the hospital held to welcome the new residents just last year. Completely put together, blond hair, blue eyes, and pearls at her neck, she was one classy girl. She had hung on his every word, and he was mesmerized by the thought that a girl like her would be interested in him. She was the kind of girl that might have asked him to help her study for her biology midterm and then wouldn't give him the time of day after the test.

It took him awhile to realize it wasn't him she wanted, just the title of "Doctor's Wife".

With Alex weighing so heavily on his mind, he had forgotten about their weekly dinner with her parents. Or maybe he had wanted to forget about it, because he had no desire to go. It would just be more of the same, and talking about it with her did no good.

He was trapped. It would be bad for his career if he broke the heart of the chief of staff's daughter. That was about the only thing he knew for sure.

He paused in front of Correspondence on his way to the train. The store was dark; only the lights in the front displays were on. They were filled with hearts and flowers, true love, that kind of thing, all to remind the romantics walking by that Valentine's Day was almost upon them.

Was Alex a romantic? he wondered. It dawned on him for the first time that there might be a boyfriend in her life, or a husband, for that matter.

The rumble of the train snapped him back to reality.

If he ran, he could probably just make it, so he broke into a jog, weaving between the few people that were out on this frigid night. His breath came out in white puffs, his cheeks heated as he picked up his pace.

Just one more person to get around and he'd be home free—he was almost to the bottom of the platform stairs.

Glancing up, he could see that the train hadn't pulled into the station yet. But he didn't see the person in front of him who had paused to set something down. A small dog on a leash dashed out in front of him. The leash pulled tight and caught him just below the knees and he fell.

He managed to twist so he didn't land on the little dog, which was on top of him, licking his face, before he even realized what had happened. The dog's owner scooped up the ugly little thing, which looked more like a hairy rat then a dog.

"I am so sorry! Are you all right? Here, let me help you up." She bent over to give him a hand, but he was laughing so hard he couldn't get up.

Above them, the train rumbled into the station and drowned out whatever she said next. When he didn't reply, she gave him a strange look and hurried away.

I must really look insane, he thought, but that made him laugh even harder.

People dashed past him, staring as they made their way up the steep stairs, but he didn't care. He sat there on the freezing pavement, laughing, as the train above him pulled away. It was some sort of strange destiny; what else explained the fact that he had tripped and fallen fifty yards from Alex's store?

He got up and brushed the snow off, turned, and walked up the steps to the train, still laughing to himself. He would come back again. This was a sign. The phone in his pocket rang again and he pulled it out, switched it off, and waited for the next train.

Chapter Five

Alex sat at her computer, trying to focus on billing for the invitations she had just printed. But she was having trouble concentrating.

The dinner with her father was still fresh in her mind. It was one of the all-time most bizarre events of her life. That he would force her shop to close by yanking the building out from under her was bad enough. But that he would do it to appease her lunatic mother—if she didn't laugh about it, she would cry.

Ignoring her social life, indecd.

It was ridiculous, but it was her reality, and she had to come up with a plan to save her shop. Just reasoning with her mother wasn't an option, not if her dad was already involved. She needed to buy herself some time.

There was a tap on the front door, and she looked up to see Claire standing there.

"Good morning, Alex!" she chirped as Alex opened the door, her limp barely noticeable thanks to the brace on her ankle. Claire's enthusiasm, which was usually infectious, was like nails on a chalkboard this morning, especially since Alex hadn't gotten her coffee yet.

"How's the ankle?"

"Fine," Alex responded.

There was so much to tell Claire, but where to begin? Peter's visit, or maybe the fact that she had fallen again, though this time on top of him? Claire would just love that. Or maybe she should just dive right into her mother's insane plan to marry her off?

Before she could tell Claire anything, the bells on the door rang again and they were joined by their friend Stephen and two styrofoam cups of coffee from the Java Bean down the street. He set one down in front of Alex and looked sheepishly at Claire.

"Didn't know you'd be here, sorry. Do you want mine? It's a vanilla latte," he said, holding the cup out to her.

Claire shook her head. "No, I'm sure it's got whipped cream and whole milk, and those are not on my diet." Claire was continually trying to lose the same five pounds, like three-fourths of the female population.

Alex had the lid off her coffee, drinking it like a man stuck in the desert would drink water, before she could think to offer hers to Claire.

"I got your message. So, what's the emergency?" Stephen asked, pushing aside the things piled up on Alex's desk to make room for himself to sit down on the corner.

"I had dinner with my dad the other night . . ." She began.

Stephen interrupted, "That is definitely an emergency. I'm surprised you didn't request a pastry to go with your coffee. How'd it go?"

"Not well," she started, limping over to sit at the chair behind her desk.

"Are you limping?"

"Oh, yeah, you gotta hear this one," Claire laughed and then launched into the story of Alex's spectacular fall with such dramatic flair that Alex actually found herself laughing along, until she got to the part about Peter.

"He stopped by here, by the way, to check my ankle and I fell again, only this time on top of him!" she interrupted, her face flushed with embarrassment. It was so ridiculous. What grown woman falls that much?

"The doctor came here to see you and you fell on him? How in the world . . ." Claire's voice trailed off in a fit of giggles.

"Yes, it was hilarious, really," Alex said dryly.

She recounted the flirting, the fall, Peter's introduction of himself to her father, and his quick exit. "I've never seen anyone stand up to my father like that, though it was easy for him to do, since he hightailed it right out of here."

"Dr. Peter Gibson," Claire's voice was dreamy. "I'd fall on him, too. If you hadn't seen him first, that is."

Alex smiled at her friend. Not one of Claire's relationships had ever lasted past the third date. It was probably because by then, she'd marked each man as her future husband.

"If it makes you feel any better, my weekend was awful, too. I ran into Katie, the girl that works at the Java Bean that I want to ask out." Stephen's eyes widened.

"Yes," Claire said, egging him on.

Well, I was happy because she told me she was so glad I was there." He paused.

"And?" Alex prodded.

"She was happy because she wanted me to meet her brother! She thinks I'm gay!" He picked a small piece of lint off his black coat and dropped it onto the floor.

Alex smiled, though in sympathy. Poor Stephen; he had the worst luck with women. He just seemed to pick the exact person that was completely wrong for him. She patted his arm to comfort him.

"Sorry," Alex said. "But I can still top you. My father is refusing to let me move the shop into his building because my mother thinks my 'little hobby' is keeping me from meeting my future husband." Shock registered on the faces of her friends. Somehow, that made her feel a little better. She filled them in on the details, even the part about her father wishing he had actually walked in on something between her and Peter.

She leaned forward and put her elbows on the desk in front of her. "So, what I need is a plan, and all I've come up with so far is for you to look at my books and see what you can come up with." She looked at Stephen, thanking her lucky stars that he was an accountant.

"In the meantime," she continued, "I'm going to go and try to make my case with my mother. Try to talk sense into her, though we all know how well that will go."

Stephen rolled his eyes while Claire sighed. They had both met her mother at the party Alex had thrown to celebrate the shop's one-year anniversary. She'd looked down her aristocratic nose at them, her hand at the pearls around her throat as she quizzed them about her daughter's love life.

"Maybe you should have seen this coming?" Claire

asked, and Alex couldn't disagree. Her lack of a love life had always concerned her mother.

"Get your books and I'll take a look," Stephen said, and Alex pulled them out of the file cabinet next to her desk.

Happily, it was almost time to open the store, and then she'd be able to focus on something else for a while. For the first time in the history of her shop, Alex was seeing her customers as revenue, and that didn't agree with her.

Stephen tucked the files into his briefcase, and then ruffled Alex's hair with his hand.

"We'll figure this out, I promise."

His optimism gave her a momentary feeling that they just might.

"I'll look these over at lunch, and then let's meet for dinner so I can let you know what I find. See you, Claire." He waved and headed for the door.

When he was gone, Claire spoke up. "So, tell me more about Doctor Perfect Teeth."

Alex almost screamed in exasperation. "Seriously, Claire, you are almost as bad as my mother!"

"No, not as bad, but your dad might have been on to something. If this guy is nice enough to come here to check on you, maybe you could get him to play along and buy you some time. It's just a thought."

When Alex stared at her in surprise, Claire backed up. "Unless you think you might actually like him and your mom would get what she wanted in the end." She stood and pulled on her coat.

"I have to run, my real job calls." Claire was a librarian at the branch around the corner.

"What do you mean by that?" Alex called after her, but Claire was out the door before she could get an answer, leaving Alex alone to ponder the insanity that was now her life.

She didn't like Peter. She didn't like anyone. Junior high girls "liked" people. They passed notes with check boxes declaring their feelings and asking if a boy felt the same.

Adults were *attracted* to people. Not that she was attracted to Peter—that wasn't it, was it? The other night she *had* been irritated that her father had interrupted them.

All right, so maybe she was attracted to him, but so what? She was human, after all, and he was obviously both incredibly handsome and incredibly caring. What wasn't to be attracted to? But she certainly didn't *like* him. Why had everyone in her life gone so insane?

She sat back down at her desk and continued working on the billing. The bells on the door chimed, and she was happy to see one of her regular customers come in. She greeted her and then went back to her work. The day passed in a flurry of customers and other work.

"When are you going to get your spring invitations in?" another one of her regulars asked.

Alex smiled at her, wondering if Correspondence would even be open for the spring showers and parties. "Soon," she said, but without conviction. Sadly, Valentine's Day might be the last holiday she was open for.

By the end of the day, she was thoroughly depressed. Even helping her customers couldn't raise her spirits.

She had just locked up for the night when the phone rang.

"Correspondence!" she said as brightly as she could into the receiver.

"Alexandria, it's Mother, dear." A familiar whisper of a voice, her mother's phone voice. The sound of it using her given name pushed her blood pressure sky high, but Alex held her tongue.

"Mother, it's such a surprise to hear from you." Sarcasm was always lost on her mother.

"After your dinner with your father, I thought you'd be expecting my call. He said you wanted to meet me for lunch at the club. How does Wednesday sound? That is my first available lunch date." She barely paused for a reply. "So, I will see you then. And, dear, please try to wear something acceptable. I look forward to hearing the news your father says will please me so much. Ta-Ta, dear." She hung up before Alex could say anything.

Her mother knew how to push all her buttons. Alex hadn't actually agreed to meet her Wednesday. She could have something that prevented her from being there. Not that she did, but she could.

Alex turned up the music and went to the Valentine craft table to straighten up. Glitter and glue were everywhere, and scraps of paper were stuck to the table. Alex sorted and cleaned, all the while singing along with the booming music—trying hard to vent her frustration, or at least burn off some energy.

When things were all straightened and re-stocked, she turned the music off and made her way to the desk. As she was shutting down the computer, she noticed the message light blinking.

Stephen's voice rang out as she pushed play. "Alex, it's me. Listen, I went over what you gave me and I haven't found anything yet. I'm going to bail on dinner and go over them again tonight. I'll call tomorrow. Hang in there!"

Alex sank down behind her desk. *Hang in there.* Not an easy task; panic was starting to rise in her throat. She really hoped Stephen would find something, anything that could help her. Nothing to do now but go home and wait for him to call her back, maybe stop and pick up some ice cream. That would help some.

As she stood and put her hand in her pocket for her mittens, her fingers felt something. Alex pulled a card out of the pocket and flipped it over to see what it was.

Dr. Peter Gibson, M.D.
312-778-2120

She flipped it around in her fingers. How desperate was she getting? Pretty darn desperate, actually. Barely hesitating, she sat down and called the number.

"Peter, it's Alex. From the other night, and the night before that, I guess. I owe you an apology for so many things. Call, me at 858-2520 and maybe we can get together tonight so I can do it in person."

Even as she punched the "off" button on the phone, that odd twittering in her stomach returned. It was official; all of it had driven her as crazy as the rest of them. How else could she explain the fact that she had just called Peter to make a date?

With nothing left to do, she switched off the lights and locked the door, pausing to look back at the shop that was her life.

Chapter Six

Alex fussed around her apartment, waiting for the phone to ring. Why had she left that message for Peter? Desperation? She went to the freezer and opened the door, stared at the various pints of ice cream inside. After a minute, she slammed it closed. She'd be irritated with herself later if she ate all the ice cream and then he actually did call.

She sat down on the couch and thumbed through the magazines she had picked up on the way home, flipping through articles with titles like "Feel Cozy, Look Flirty," and "Five Things Every Woman Should Know About Nail Polish." None of it held her interest. She turned to the astrology page; at least her horoscope intrigued her.

Capricorns generally come up with the perfect witty answer one day too late. Impulse and intuition take a back seat to their excellent self-control. The day ahead is an opportunity to let go of the inhibitions that characterize you. Yield to your

instincts a little and see what occurs. A little more
socializing wouldn't hurt, either. Even Capricorns
are entitled to some fun now and then. . . .

Now wasn't that fitting! It couldn't be truer at this
moment.

The bells on her front door jangled—Milo wanted to
go out. When she had gotten her beloved dog, she had
been adamant he would not be "a four legged
yapper"—some small dogs could make more noise
than a dump truck. So she had tied some bells to the
front doorknob that hung at Milo's level. When he had
to go out, he simply pushed at them with his nose, and
they were both happy.

Pleased with the distraction, Alex grabbed her coat
and Milo's leash. They walked the sidewalks in her
neighborhood toward the dog park. With the brace that
Peter had given her, her ankle barely registered on her
pain scale. Though it was pretty stiff, she barely even
limped.

The park was a good time-killer; however, it did
mean that she wouldn't be home to answer the phone if
Peter called. She let Milo off his leash and found a
bench to sit and wait while he did his business and
played some with the other dogs.

Her obsession with Peter was beginning to be a little
troubling for her. She couldn't really decide why she
wanted him to call. Was it that he could help her distract her mother, or was it more?

In the appearance department, he was something
indeed, and he was somewhat interested in her, or at
least she thought he might be. After all, he had come to

her store, hadn't just called. Physical attraction, that's all it was. She just hadn't experienced it in such a long time that it was hard to recognize. Besides, if she was dwelling on him, she didn't have to think about her other problems . . . and there were many.

She whistled for Milo, who was chasing after a German shepherd. He ran all-out toward her. When he reached her, she knelt down, scratched his ears, and clipped his leash onto his collar. "A little out of your league there, aren't you?"

The light on her answering machine was not flashing when they returned. Not a good sign. Soon she would have to let go of the notion that she was going out that night. The TV held little promise, and the magazines were not intriguing to her. *What to do to kill time?* She marched herself into the bathroom and looked in the mirror.

She pulled her hair back so she could get a closer look, inching near to the mirror. She hadn't been sleeping well, but her new concealer seemed to be taking care of the black circles under her eyes. Her eyebrows, however, were out of control. Somewhere she remembered reading an article on the new trend for eyebrow shape.

She went to the basket beside her bed and flipped through the stack until the title caught her eye: "New Eyebrow Shapes That Will Stop Them in Their Tracks." There it was on the cover of *Glamour. This will kill some time,* she thought to herself.

She pulled out her tweezers and began yanking out the hairs. Wincing at every pluck, she worked furiously, until she looked at the counter to see it covered with tiny black hairs. She stepped back and admired her work. Not bad. For once, her eyebrows were even and the same size.

Then she opened the medicine cabinet and scanned its contents, still looking for something to do.

She pulled out a tube full of mud mask and applied it to her face, being careful, as the tube instructed, to avoid her eyes and mouth—though she did manage to get it up one of her nostrils. She sneezed and then decided that it was never going to be applied as perfectly as it appeared on the women on the tube, but it was close enough. Now it had to dry.

What to do while it did? That was the question. She considered deep conditioning her hair, but that would be admitting defeat—there would be no time to dry *and* style it if Peter called. A bath would be relaxing, but the steam would do a number on her hair, too. A pedicure was the obvious answer. She pulled off her socks to look at the damage she had done to her professional pedicure when she fell. The polish was chipped, but the nails themselves were still perfectly even. All she had to do was apply some fresh polish. She removed the old and then stuck cotton balls between her toes and went to work applying Peek-a-boo Pink. That done, she walked awkwardly into her bedroom.

The clock on her bedside table said 7:00 P.M.; almost two hours had passed since she left the message for Peter. Why in the world did she think he would call her back? Obviously, she had gotten herself all worked up for no reason. He had merely been doing his duty as a doctor when he checked on her. Any interest she had perceived on his part was strictly professional.

The freezer called out to her; it was going to be at

least a two-pint night. She would start with Chubby
Hubby and move on from there. She opened the draw-
er and found it empty. All her spoons were in the sink,
a clear indication of what life had been like the last few
days. It was just one more thing to worry about on her
long list. She winced. Soon she could either be poor, or,
if her mother had her way, wearing Ralph Lauren and
pearls. Both options frightened her.

The phone rang just as she was putting the first
spoonful into her mouth. Its piercing sound caused her
to jump up from her place on the couch, where she had
settled in to watch *Behind the Music: the Go-Gos.*

"Hello?" She tried to swallow before she answered,
but the result was a garbled version of the greeting.

"Alex?" Peter sounded nervous, and she felt butter-
flies in her stomach at the sound of his voice.

She swallowed the remaining ice cream. "Yes?" she
said awkwardly.

"Hi. I got your message, but I didn't have time to call
you back, so . . ."

Alex interrupted him. "That's okay; it was late
notice. I took a chance that you wouldn't be busy.
Maybe another time?" She tried not to let her disappointment show in her voice.

"No, what I started to say was, I didn't have to time
to call you when I got off work so I just jumped on
the El. I'm at the stop near your shop. Do you live
nearby?"

Her eyes scanned her apartment—magazines strewn
on the floor, her bed unmade. She shuddered to think of
the state she had left the bathroom in. To most people
it was a little messy, but to her, it looked as though a
tornado had come through.

"Yes, very close actually, but how about if I meet you at Izzy's, the bar right past the El stop?"

"Sure, I know the place. See you in a few minutes?"

She walked into the bathroom and looked at her ragged appearance. "Better make it at least fifteen minutes. See you there."

After hanging up, she washed off the mask, splashing cold water up from the sink in an attempt to speed up the process, though the instructions clearly stated that she should wipe it away in a circular motion with a warm soft cloth. Her face looked exactly as it had before she started.

On went her make-up and down came her hair. She pulled the cotton balls from between her toes and covered the still damp polish with socks. She'd deal with the repercussions of that later.

She chose the same clothes she had worn to work that day—hip huggers and one of those peasant blouses, wrinkled slightly because she hadn't taken the time to hang them up. If she had to pick out a new outfit, it would take at least half an hour.

When she was through, she barely paused to look in the mirror as she grabbed her coat and purse and rushed out the door. Not bad, not too overdone, but still, she looked pretty good, if she did say so herself.

On the street, the cold slowed her pace, and she had a moment to analyze how she was feeling. Claire had been ridiculous to suggest using Peter to run interference with her mother. She wouldn't even entertain the idea—mostly because it would be buying into her mother's crazy plan.

However, she had to admit Claire was right about one

thing: Alex was extremely attracted to the good doctor. The thought of his dark blue eyes warmed her against the freezing Chicago wind. Yes, this would be just the distraction she needed.

Chapter Seven

Alex opened the door to the dimly lit bar and her eyes scanned the room, looking for him. *Not at the bar, not at the tables in the front.* She walked through until she found him, sitting at one of the booths in the back. He was wearing a blue shirt that set off those eyes, and, of course, he was smiling.

"Hey," she said, taking off her coat and sliding into the booth across from him. A beer sat on the table in front of him and before he could say anything, a waitress appeared to take her order. After requesting a martini, she glanced up to find that he was still looking at her.

"Hey, yourself. That was less than ten minutes. You either live right above this place or your ankle is feeling better." He winked.

She blushed. "Oh, the ankle, it's coming along nicely. I think the wrap really has helped. Thanks for that."

Her drink came, and she took a sip, not sure what to say next. She was really bad at this, making small talk.

She liked to get right to the point, but in this situation she wasn't quite sure which point she wanted to get to.

"So," he said, obviously waiting for her to say something important. She had invited him, after all.

"Hm," she replied, wishing she could get to the point . . . any point. "I need to apologize for my father. He has no idea how rude he is." There, she needed to tell him that anyway.

"Well, any man would be a little bit upset to discover his daughter in that position, I would think. I'm sure his bark is worse than his bite." He sat back in the booth, draping his arm along the back of the seat. "I was surprised to get your message. I was pretty sure I was annoying you."

"Let's just say there are more annoying things in my life than you at the moment. My father included." She looked at him sheepishly. "I was pretty rude to you, myself. I was surprised you returned my call, let alone agreed to meet me."

"Are you kidding? The first two times I've been in your company, you have fallen down twice, once on top of me. I can hardly wait to see what happens this time." He laughed.

What a great laugh. Alex was briefly alarmed. He seemed so perfect. Great looks, a sense of humor, compassion—what was he hiding?

"I plan to remain seated throughout our entire date in order to avoid the inevitable. You probably need a night off from patching me up anyway. So what kind of doctor are you?"

Please don't say "dermatologist," please don't say "dermatologist," she thought to herself. The thought of him studying moles on old ladies and the bad skin of teenage boys didn't mesh with the idea of him she had conjured up in her head.

"Well, I'm finishing the second year of my residency in Emergency Room Medicine. I'm hoping to stay on at Mercy Hospital. I have a chance at becoming Chief ER Resident, so we'll see."

Relieved, Alex said, "Well, once you're done with your residency, that's when you can start making the big bucks . . . That's what you doctors aspire to—right?"

Peter's eyes narrowed. "Actually, no. What I really want to do is open a small family practice." He shifted in his seat, staring directly at her. The change in his demeanor was evident. "I'm not really interested in the whole affluent doctor lifestyle. I don't golf, or sail, or any of that."

"So you got into medicine to *help people*?" Her voice registered the shock. Maybe she wasn't the only person in the world whose main goal in life was to make money.

He nodded. "However, right now I'm swimming in student loans, so I think of that as a long-term goal for myself." The waitress set a bowl of peanuts on the table. He took some and popped them into his mouth.

"So, just so I understand. You put yourself through medical school, incurred a great deal of debt, so you can help people?" Alex was incredulous. *Good looks and a good person, too. What are the chances of that?*

"Let me guess, some doctor saved your life or the life of your brother and it inspired you to do greater good?" She helped herself to the peanuts.

"I think maybe you've seen too many made-for-TV movies. I just like helping people. I'm pretty good at it.

I like the process of diagnosing, taking my hints from my patients and their symptoms, and then telling them what to do to feel better. Like you and your ankle. It gives me a great feeling of satisfaction." He shrugged. "It's important that people have a passion for what they do, I think. Like you, for instance. Are you passionate about greeting cards?"

Passionate about greeting cards? It seemed a bit ridiculous the way he said it, but she was passionate about her work.

"Well, the thing about Correspondence is that it's more of a philosophy than a shop. That's why I opened it in the first place."

"A philosophy? I'm intrigued," he said, tilting his head to the side and looking at her intently. For the first time Alex felt like she could tell someone how she felt about her shop, without feeling self-conscious about it.

"I just feel that the most important factor in a relationship is communication. That goes for any relationship, not just the romantic kind—siblings, parent-child, friendships—all of them. Telling people what you think and feel—that's important. I wanted to create a place where people could find what they are looking for to express themselves. Not just fit what they are thinking into whatever Hallmark card is close enough."

She sat, waiting for the inevitable chuckle about placing so much importance on something so mundane, but when it didn't come, she looked up.

"Wow, that's pretty profound. I never thought about it that way. So, are you finding people that agree? I mean, are you successful at it?"

"Not as successful as my dad would like."

"What does he have to do with it? I mean, my parents would have been fine if I chose to bag groceries close to home, but they're happy because I'm happy."

Alex ran her fingers across the worn table, pausing in the grooves. "Well, that would be the difference between my parents and normal people. My dad helped me negotiate the rent on my shop, but the lease is up this spring and the landlord wants more money. So, my father bought a new retail space and I was supposed to move my shop into it. However, now my mother, who has way too much money and time on her hands, has decided I should be spending more of my time finding a husband. So she's making my dad refuse to rent me the new space." Every time she told the story, it seemed more ridiculous than the last.

"Are you kidding?" He threw back his head and laughed. "What is this, the eighteenth century?"

"That is exactly what I thought! So now, I need to figure out a way to convince my mother she is wrong, which is about as likely as Cubs and White Sox fans agreeing. I have my work cut out for me."

He shook his head, and at that moment they both reached for the peanuts, their fingertips barely touching, and Alex felt herself get warm all over.

Peter knew the moment his fingers touched Alex's that he was in trouble. Who was he kidding to think he could come and meet her for a casual drink and then head back to the drudgery that had become his daily life? He hadn't stopped thinking about her since they met.

When he'd gotten her message, he had run out of the hospital and caught the first train up here, not even pausing to think about what it would mean to be sitting across the table from her.

He looked up from the bowl and met her gaze. She hadn't moved her hand away. What did that mean? He cleared his throat.

Peter pulled his own hand away. "Listen, I have early rounds tomorrow, so I should probably call it a night. Can I walk you home?"

She looked confused, and then pulled her hand back, tucking it into her lap. "Sure. I mean, I just live around the corner, but yeah. I'd like that." She got up and grabbed her coat. Rummaging through her purse, she pulled out a small change purse containing a small wad of bills. She uncrumpled them and put a few on the table before he could figure out what she was doing.

"I'll get that," he said reaching for his wallet. He'd had enough of someone else paying for his drinks. Ashleigh would just whip out Daddy's credit card and insist on paying. He handed Alex her money back before she could protest and laid down his own.

"Thanks," she said, meeting his gaze. "Ready?"

He followed her out of the bar. The men on either side of the tight aisle turned to look at Alex as she passed. Though she didn't seem to notice, it wasn't lost on Peter.

He opened the door and held it for her. "I'd feel much better if you would hold onto my arm. No telling how much damage you could do to yourself out here on the ice." He took her hand and put it on his elbow.

Playing with fire, that's what he was doing. He knew that until he resolved things with Ashleigh, nothing could come of this. And resolving things with Ashleigh would take some doing. But somehow he couldn't help himself.

He followed Alex's lead down a side street, both of them silent until finally she spoke.

"I really had a good time tonight, and that's unusual for me. I don't really date." She laughed, and then her cheeks, already pink from the cold night air, deepened to a shade of red. "Sorry, I didn't mean that the way it sounded."

"You don't date?" He was shocked. "Ever?" His pulse quickened. This cleared up his question about a boyfriend.

She shook her head. "I find dating to be a waste of time. No offense to your gender, but men aren't always the most honest people."

He laughed. "No offense taken, but in defense of my gender as a whole, sometimes women aren't exactly easy to figure out."

"That's a good point. I try to dispel that rumor by just being myself and not beating around the bush."

They came to an abrupt stop in front of her building. "You want to come in?" she asked, turning toward him. It was all he wanted, but he knew he couldn't do it. Being a man of integrity had its downfalls.

"Thanks, but I have those early rounds." It sounded lame even to him. And he kicked himself that he couldn't come up with anything more original.

Her eyes dimmed. "Yeah, right, I forgot. Well, thanks for coming all the way up here." At least she sounded disappointed, that was something.

She turned to go upstairs but then stopped, and came close to him. She laid her hands on his cheeks and looked into his eyes.

"Like I said, I don't beat around the bush." Then she kissed him. It was a kiss like he'd never had before, her lips soft and warm. He let his arms go around her, pull her closer to him. Knowing it was wrong, he still couldn't stop himself.

She stepped back, seemingly flustered.

"I can't believe I did that." She hid her face in her hands. "I get to the point, but I usually don't throw myself at a guy who has already said he didn't want to come in. I don't know what I was thinking."

"Sometimes thinking things through can stop you from getting what you want," he said, pulling her hands from her cheeks. "And I never said I didn't *want* to come in. I said I *couldn't* come in—two completely different things."

He pulled her close and held her to him. "I had a great time tonight. You are like no one I have ever met in my life."

"And that's a good thing?" She laughed into his chest.

"More than you know. It's just, my life isn't my own right now. Being a resident, and all that comes with it." He thought of Ashleigh and all she came with. "It doesn't leave me much free time."

She stepped back from him. "You didn't think I was looking for some big commitment, did you? That's not it at all. I had a great time tonight, and I thought that maybe we could hang out a little longer. Believe me, the last thing I am looking for is some big committed relationship." Her green eyes, watery from the cold, looked back at him. "Call me when you have time. I liked just talking to you tonight." Was that surprise he heard in her voice?

"I will. I liked talking to you, too. And we'll have to discuss that kiss."

She turned, walking up the stairs to her building. "Yeah, that was some kiss." She unlocked the door and went inside, turning to wave. Then she was gone.

He stood for a minute in the cold. That *was* some kiss, and as he turned to walk back toward the train, he knew one thing for certain. He couldn't wait to do it again.

Chapter Eight

All around her, waiters in crisp white shirts and black bow ties swarmed, as if they were performing some sort of strange ballet. Alex pulled nervously at her skirt, covering her knees. What had she been thinking this morning when she chose this outfit?

Her mind flashed back to the scene at her apartment that morning. Every single item of clothing she owned strewn around her bedroom—shirts, skirts, pants, shoes. Her current ensemble had been the winner. However, at this moment she couldn't remember why for the life of her. It was not going to make a good impression on her mother.

Not that anything she wore would make a difference, unless it was a nice sweater set with pearls. No, here at the East Bank Club, her mother's club, Alex stood out like a sore thumb in her short print skirt and blouse. Nevertheless, it was the most conservative thing she owned.

The distraction had been nice, though. It had given

her something to focus on other than constantly replaying her evening with Peter. Two things about that night bothered her. One, that she had thrown herself at him, and two, that she had enjoyed being with him, a lot.

The first she could write off to a combination of martinis and how incredibly handsome and charming he had been. Not to mention that horoscope she had read. She was sure she never would have done such a thing without that potent combination of things.

She couldn't get her mind around the second thing, enjoying his company so much. That evening played repeatedly in her mind. She couldn't stop thinking about Peter, and not just his physical appearance, but also the way he spoke, the feeling inside her when she sat across from him at the table, everything about him.

Every empty second, from when she woke up to when she'd fallen asleep, she had focused on their evening. She found herself getting a flutter in her stomach and her palms sweating. Alex, of all people, couldn't process what was going on. She'd never experienced it before. She suspected Peter could be the person that could change her mind about romance, but the timing was awful. She had to focus on running her business and figuring out how to keep it open.

"This is ridiculous," she muttered to herself. It would have been just as effective if she hadn't showed up at all. Once her mother made up her mind about something, nothing was going to change it. Then she thought of Correspondence and resigned herself to her mission: to make her mother see it was worthwhile for the store to stay open—whatever it took.

As if on cue, her mother floated across the dining room. Immaculate in her linen pantsuit, her ever-present pearls around her neck, her blond hair perfectly cut in her signature bob. Her mother was a beautiful woman; there was no arguing that. Heads turned as she made her way through the sea of tables and chairs and arrived where Alex sat.

"Alexandria." She motioned for Alex to stand up, and when she did, they embraced stiffly. Her mother leaned forward as if to kiss her, but her pink lips never actually touched Alex's cheek, stopping just short.

Alex went to sit back down and her mother frowned briefly, leaving Alex to wonder what she could have done wrong already. Aside from the outfit, that is. Magically, two waiters appeared and held out their chairs. Alex nodded, making a mental note of her misstep.

Being with her mother was always the same for Alex. They did their same little dance, each of them moving out of the way of the other. It should bother her more, Alex knew, but this was her relationship with her mother. It wasn't as though this was something new. Her mother had no interest in the person Alex was, only in turning her into the daughter she always wanted. That was never going to happen. Therefore, the rest of the dance was just for show.

"That is an interesting outfit, dear." Her mother said as she unfolded the white napkin in front of her and placed it in her lap. Alex did the same, biting back the first sarcastic quip that came to her. Attacking her mother was not the way to go. Instead, she decided to take it as a compliment—throw her mom off her game a little if she could.

"Thank you. And you look as lovely as always, Mother."

Who said that? Whose sticky sweet voice paid that compliment? Alex almost looked over her shoulder to check, but then, when her mother smiled, she felt a glimmer of hope that she could win her over. Her portfolio sat in the chair beside her; she was reaching for it to show her mother the proof that the shop was doing well when one of the waiters appeared with glasses of ice tea.

Her mother reached for hers as she spoke, squeezing the lemon against her spoon. "So, your father tells me that you have some sort of surprise for me?"

"Surprise, no, but I do have the invitations I did for Mimi Sutherby's bridal shower." Alex grasped her portfolio in her hand and opened it to the first page. She held it across the table for her mother to see.

The Sutherbys were her parents' best friends. Mimi was the exact daughter her mother wanted—she had learned to play bridge and do the waltz. She had gone to college, but only to earn her MRS. Degree. Now she was getting married, just as she should in the world Alex's mother lived in. All was right in the Sutherby house, and Susan Sanders was going to try to put things right in her house, too. Before it was too late.

Alex regretted starting with this invitation immediately. She wished she could reach across and grab the book back from her mother, but there wasn't any need, because her mother wasn't looking at it. She closed the book and set it back on the chair where it had been sitting.

"Alexandria, this little shop of yours—I thought your

father was going to speak to you about it. Leave it to Howard to forget such an important thing," she said, rolling her eyes.

"He didn't forget. We talked about it at dinner last week. That's why I wanted to have lunch with you, to show you how well the shop is doing and . . ."

Her mother waved her hands in front of her, a flick of the wrist to dismiss what Alex was saying, and Alex's blood pressure started to rise.

"We never should have indulged you with that shop in the first place. It's time for you to settle down and get serious about your social standing in life—you need to focus on finding a husband."

That was it. The small grasp Alex held on her temper snapped. "*Standing?* You cannot be serious. Mother, this is not the eighteenth century. My *standing* is fine. I am happy, not to mention successful. I don't need to find a husband to be happy. You apparently need me to find a husband to be happy!" She shook with anger, and she reached for her tea to try to calm herself down before this got any worse.

"Dear, this tone you are using is so unflattering." Her mother looked around the room to see if anyone had noticed, and was visibly relieved to see that no one had. "Now, please let's talk about something sensible." She paused as the waiter approached the table with two plates of salad, which he set in front of them.

Alex was confused. She started to wave the waiter away; he must have the wrong table.

"I took the liberty of ordering for us," her mother said breezily.

"Mother, I am perfectly capable of ordering for

myself," Alex whined. *Why, when I'm with my mother, do I suddenly start acting like a child?*, she wondered.

"Nonsense, I eat here practically every day, I know what is good and what isn't. Don't whine, Alexandria, it's so unbecoming."

She acted like a child because she was being treated like one. That was the first thing that made sense since she'd gotten to this place.

"Now, about this surprise your father was talking about. He implied that it involved your love life. Do tell—perhaps we are more on the same page then you have let on." She took a forkful of her salad and raised it to her pink lips.

That was all Alex could take. Her mother had brushed off how successful the shop was, ordered her lunch, scolded her voice and her clothing, and now she wouldn't drop the whole "surprise" thing. There was no surprise. But there was Peter. It crossed Alex's mind to tell her mother about him. No, that would be doing exactly what she wanted, and Alex refused to do that.

So instead, she did what any sane daughter in her position would do. She excused herself to the ladies room. Crossing the room, she focused first on her feet, one in front of the other, no limp evident. Then the door that lead to the lobby where the bathrooms were.

She pushed on it and it swung out, knocking the tray out of the hands of a waiter who was just about to come through. She looked at the mess and then at the door. Darn it, wrong door, this one led to the kitchen. The lobby door was down farther, closer to the windows.

What was with her and waiters? The noise was deafening as the dishes, piled high with food, crashed onto the marble floor. Lucky for her, the door swung closed before she could see the expression on her mother's face. She knelt to try to help, but the waiter waved her off. Before she could bat an eye, five identically dressed young men appeared to help clean up, all of them apologizing *to her.*

Unbelievable.

"Please stop apologizing; it was my fault." She looked at the waiters, who seemed somewhat shocked that she was talking to them, let alone apologizing. Then again, they were used to dealing with people like her mother. Any sincerity or gesture of kindness was foreign to them, especially during the lunch hour.

"Okay, if you won't let me help, could one of you at least tell me how to get to the bathroom without going back into the dining room?" she asked as she stood up.

One of them pointed toward a door on the other side of the room. She stepped over the pile of broken dishes and food, carefully. All she needed was to slip in the spill and fall on one of them.

Through the door and into the lobby, she made her way into the ladies room, pausing in the lounge area with relief. Looking around, she almost laughed. It was both bigger and nicer than her apartment. She sat down on the couch to collect herself. Some of her anger had been replaced with embarrassment about the tray, but just picturing her mother's face made it all come back to her.

What was she going to do? It was clear her mother did not intend to listen to reason. Stephen hadn't come up with anything yet. All of her cash was tied up in inventory and orders for the spring season. He'd felt so bad that he had brought her coffee and a scone when he came by to tell her. He had some ideas, but she wasn't holding out hope.

She felt like banging her head against the wall, literally. But she'd already made quite a scene and she knew if she did anything of the kind, someone would see her and before she knew it her mother would have her committed.

She went to the mirror and frowned at her reflection. Her face was blotchy and her lipstick a little smeared, not the face of success. She pulled her compact from her purse and went to work, then blotted her lipstick with a tissue. She was cramming it all back in her purse when her cell phone rang.

"Alex Sanders," she said as she flipped it open.

"Alex, listen, I just have a minute, but I think I may have found an answer to your problem. I was flipping through *Chicago* magazine and there is an ad for the Spring Bridal fair." Claire was talking so fast that she was hard to understand.

"Claire, booths there cost a fortune. I don't have the money for that." Alex sighed. There was no solution. Nothing was going to save her.

"I've got that covered. Don't worry, we'll talk about it when you get back from your lunch. You just need to buy some time with you mom. The show is in three weeks. That's all the time we need. Just don't fight with her, keep it light and get out. Oh, and Stephen called— he says he has good news, too. I'll meet you at the shop in one hour." With that, she hung up.

What was Claire up to? And what was Stephen's news? Alex stood staring at her phone. Only Claire would drop that bombshell and hang up.

It was too late. She'd already had the fight with her

mother. Kissing up now was out of the question. Maybe she could play up this surprise her mom kept talking about—be evasive keep her on her toes. But never answer any direct questions. Obviously, her mom thought it was a man she was keeping secret, and a man it would have to be.

She breezed back into the dining room, her head high, smiling. This had to work; whatever Claire was up to with this Bridal Show, it just had to be the answer.

Just as she reached the table, she stopped short. Her mother sat facing her, across the table from a man whose back looked vaguely familiar. Obviously, she was taking Alex's love life into her own hands. Alex shuddered at the thought of who her mother was trying to fix her up with—probably some geeky stock broker or tax attorney. All the sons of her parents' friends were so boring, they thought yawning was some kind of compliment.

"Focus, calm down," Alex muttered to herself, as she approached the table. Her jaw dropped. The man sitting across from her mother was Peter.

"Alex, dear, you did have a surprise for me after all," her mother said, her voice low and charming, the complete opposite of the tone she had been using earlier. "I've just met your doctor friend. Isn't he just something else?" She patted Alex's hand as she sat—fell, really—in her chair.

"Yes, he's something else, all right." Alex muttered, then turned on her best smile, unsure what to do next.

Chapter Nine

Wen Peter first thought he saw Alex walking forcefully across the dining room at the East Bank Club, he chalked it up to merely his subconscious conjuring her up. He had been thinking so much about her that now he was sure he saw her everywhere. But when he heard the clamor of dishes from the kitchen door, he realized it must really be her. When he thought about it, the woman did have a bit of a limp.

Ashleigh had asked him to meet her for lunch and he'd agreed, thinking it would be a good time for him to try once again to convince her he wasn't the man for her. It had been on his mind for such a long time, and he was tired of racking his brain to think of the best way to do it. She had to see they just weren't headed in the same direction, that she wanted different things in her life than he did. For example, he looked forward to his volunteer hours at the clinic on the west side. The closest Ashleigh came to helping others was donating last season's wardrobe to the hospital auxiliary.

No, they definitely were not a matched set, and that was what he planned to tell her. Unfortunately, Ashleigh had other ideas for their lunch. As soon as he'd sat down, after settling her into her chair, she'd bombarded him with her not-so-subtle hints.

"So, we have to make this a quick lunch, darling, I am meeting my cousin Kate to look for *bridesmaid's* dresses." Her emphasis was clear. Peter knew they were definitely not on the same page.

"Listen, Ashleigh, we need to talk, seriously, about our future. I think . . ."

"Oh, Peter! I know. It's such an exciting time for both of us. I can hardly wait to talk about it." She unfolded her napkin, and smiled at him coyly. "But today I simply must meet Kate at Margie's Bridal Salon. I just have time for a quick bite." Magically, the waiter appeared with menus and iced tea.

Peter took a moment to survey the menu. All he could think about as he looked around this classy club was the dark booth in the back of the tavern in Lincoln Park. He wanted peanuts and beer. He sighed. "I'll take the chicken sandwich."

Ashleigh ordered the Cobb salad, making some remark about having to maintain her figure. As if her daily workout with Lars, her trainer, wouldn't be enough to keep her thin. She was talking about the bridesmaid dresses. Again.

What attracted me to her in the first place? Peter wondered.

The answer to that was actually quite simple, he knew. Back then, it was the mere fact that someone like her could be interested in someone like him. How he wished he had paid closer attention to her motives. If

he had been thinking clearly, he never would have gotten himself into this situation. Not that there was anything wrong with Ashleigh; she would make someone a
wonderful wife, just not him.

"Don't forget that Daddy wants to see you this afternoon in his office." She smiled; her blue eyes sparkled
with excitement. "This day is an important one for both
of us."

It was as if she could read his mind. Bringing her
father into it, as if to remind him what breaking up with
her could cost him. Peter sighed. It probably wasn't a
good idea to break her heart and then meet with the
chief of staff, not if he wanted to keep his job anyway.
Better to make her see that the guy she was looking at
in her dream life wasn't him. Ashleigh breaking up
with him, amicably, was his only way out. He just needed a little time to come up with a plan.

Their food came and he somehow managed to make
small talk as he ate—mostly questions about her
friends and family, what upcoming social events she
was attending. Then, as quickly as she arrived,
Ashleigh was up and ready to get to the bridal shop.

"I must go. You go ahead and finish your lunch, darling. Just give them Daddy's number, you know it by
now."

He began to reply that he could pay for his own lunch
but before he could speak, she was standing next to
him, bending down, her breath warm on his ear.

"You have a good meeting. Tell Daddy hello!" She
kissed him on the cheek and then wiped the mark from
her lipstick away. "I'll be thinking of the day I get to
pick out my own dresses the entire time I'm there," she
whispered in his ear, her breath warm. Then she turned

and walked across the room, pausing several times to wave at women she knew.

Peter pushed his plate away. He'd lost his appetite. What could he do to make Ashleigh think it was in her best interests to end things?

That was when he saw Alex. She stood at a table in the corner across the room. Then he watched as she limped across the room and into the kitchen. After the horrendous noise of the tray falling, he followed her. His few experiences with Alex had taught him that where she went, someone needing medical attention might follow.

The door to the kitchen swung shut, and he peeked in to see her kneeling next to a pile of food and broken dishes, her mouth moving quickly—apologizing, he was sure. Then she was gone, through a side door.

What was it with her and waiters? What was she doing here, for that matter? He moved back to his own table, barely avoiding his own run-in with a waiter who was balancing a tray of salads.

How many heads of lettuce did this place go through in one lunch?

Alex was meeting her mother. That was why she was here. Today was the day she was trying to convince her mother to keep her store open.

The image of Alex lying on top of him, both of them staring up at her father, flashed in his mind. At the time, he hadn't thought about the need to make a good impression, since he hadn't gotten to know Alex yet. He hadn't put his arms around her slim waist and pulled her close as she kissed him. That kiss, warm and sweet, had gone right through him. What's more, as had become the norm in the last few days, when he thought of it, he couldn't stop thinking about how perfect a moment it had been.

With her mother, he had a clean slate. He picked up the spoon from his table and tried to catch his reflection in it, like he had seen people do on television. However, all he saw was a funhouse-mirror version of himself, his head rather large, and his body small. Everything out of proportion, but he could see that his hair was, for the most part, in place. He set it back on the table and checked to see if Alex had returned to her table.

She hadn't. He should probably wait for her to reappear, he thought, glancing at his watch. Rounds started in half an hour and he couldn't be late for his meeting. Maybe he could go out to the lobby and see what was keeping her? Or maybe just stop by the table and introduce himself to her mother as a friend of Alex's, and that would be that. After all, as far as he knew, Alex had left the restaurant.

Peter walked across the room, careful to avoid any waiters, and found himself standing next to the table of a beautiful, older woman.

"Mrs. Sanders, I wanted to introduce myself, I'm a friend of your daughter's." He smiled at her and she set her fork down on her plate.

She looked up at him, shock registering on her perfectly made-up face. "Well, now, this is a pleasant surprise. Do sit down and join me." She motioned to the chair beside her.

"I have to get back to the hospital, I have rounds . . ." Peter objected.

"Rounds? You're a doctor, then. Well, I must say, Alexandria certainly has done a splendid job of surprising me." She laughed, a polite tittering really, and extended her hand across the table. "Susan Sanders. And you are?"

"Peter Gibson, Mrs. Sanders, I am pleased to meet you." He shook her hand gently. The large diamond on her ring finger practically blinded him. Not knowing what else to do, he slid into the chair next to her.

"Alexandria failed to mention how incredibly handsome you are. Actually, she failed to mention you at all. That is to be expected of her, unfortunately. When did the two of you start dating?"

Peter cleared his throat; this was not going as planned. Dating? Alexandria? Surprise? He'd thought Alex was being dramatic when she described her mother, but clearly she knew her mother well. He needed to get out, before he said something he shouldn't.

Her eyes looked past him as he started to excuse himself, and Peter shifted in his chair, feeling suddenly as though he had done something wrong.

"Alex, dear, you did have a surprise for me after all! I've just met your doctor friend. Isn't he just something else?" She patted Alex's hand as she sat—fell, really—in her chair.

"Yes, he's something else, all right," Alex replied, her voice tight as she turned her wide-eyed gaze to Peter. He smiled and shrugged, still unsure what was going on.

"You do have a flair for the dramatic, darling. Bringing those silly invitations and insisting there was no one in your life. Then, well, to call *Dr.* Gibson anything but fabulous would be an understatement! Where did the two of you meet?"

Peter looked down, directing his eyes from what he anticipated to be a heated response from Alex. This wasn't his idea of a good first impression. Her mother loved him, but based on the look on Alex's face, it wasn't going to matter much.

"Peter and I met at a charity event a few weeks ago." Alex set her hand on top of his and Peter's mouth fell open in shock. He met her gaze, perplexed, but she smiled at him so sweetly that there wasn't anything he could do but go along with whatever game she was playing. He placed his hand on top of hers, trying to ignore the shock of pleasure that came from just touching her again.

"You caught me, mother. I was trying to surprise you, and now that my surprise is out, I want to tell everyone about this wonderful man." Her voice sounded so much like her mother's. The transformation was both remarkable and creepy, in Peter's opinion.

Peter smiled back at her. It was probably in his best interests to let her do all the talking, since he didn't have a clue what was going on.

"Well, it is a most unexpected and pleasant surprise. And a charity event, no less! Perhaps you understand your place in our society more then I had anticipated."

"Yes, perhaps I do," Alex responded.

Suddenly Peter realized what Alex was doing—giving her mother what she wanted, and the woman was playing right into it. Alex hadn't lost her mind. She was doing what she'd planned—saving Correspondence.

"That is one of the many things I find so interesting about Alex, her willingness to help others." Peter chimed in. "Like her shop—most people would think it was just another card store, but not with Alex in charge. With her help, people get something special, exactly what they want, even if they weren't sure what they wanted." He reached across the table and touched her cheek, looking deep into her eyes. As she smiled back at him, he almost forgot it was all an act.

"Yes, but now, with you demanding I close the shop, Mother, where in the world will Mimi Sutherby get her invitations at the last minute?" Alex asked as she coyly lifted her iced tea and took a drink, leaving one hand on top of Peter's.

"What are you talking about, dear? Aren't you doing those invitations? You just showed them to me." Susan waved her hand in the direction of the portfolio that sat in the only empty chair at the table. "Close the shop, indeed. Cassandra Sutherby called just this morning to say how wonderful she thought they were. And now I can call her back and tell her all about your Peter."

She took the napkin from her lap and laid it beside her plate. "I am so sorry, but I do have to run. I have another commitment this afternoon. I am so very busy, never a free moment," she tittered.

Their check appeared and she signed with a flourish. "However, I will have to find time for you and Peter to come to the house for dinner. I'm sure your father will be as happy as I am to get to know him better."

Peter thought again about the first time he had met Mr. Sanders, and doubted very much that the man wanted to do anything of the sort. However, based on this bizarre lunch, he was beginning to think anything was possible with the Sanders family.

Susan rose from the table and bent to kiss her daughter on the cheek, stopping just short, he noticed.

"The two of you stay, enjoy yourselves, and I will call you to set up that dinner. Peter, it was delightful to meet you." She moved around the table and he stood to shake her hand, but she leaned over and kissed him, this time landing on her target, not pausing just above his mouth. This day just got stranger and stranger.

"Ta-ta," she said, and then she was gone. It struck Peter how similar her walk across the dining room was to Ashleigh's earlier one.

He sat back down and reached across the crisp white tablecloth for Alex's hand, which she quickly withdrew and placed in her lap.

"What in the world are you doing here?" she asked, shaking her head in disbelief.

"Well, apparently, I'm here to surprise the mother of my new girlfriend. We work pretty well together, if I do say so myself." He smiled at her, but she didn't smile back.

"Peter, you have no idea what you are getting yourself into here. We need to think this through. I mean, my mother thinks you and I are a *couple*. I can't even wrap my mind around this." She was talking so fast, so wildly, that Peter thought she might start to hyperventilate.

"How hard can it be to fool your parents?" Peter said, grabbing hold of one of her hands in an attempt to calm her down. "If you'll remember, we did have a date the other night that went pretty well. Besides, she gave you what you wanted—you get to keep the shop open."

And you and I can spend time together, he thought to himself.

That did indeed settle Alex down. She took a big drink of her water, sat back in her chair, and reached across the table for her portfolio.

"On some level, I'm mad at myself. I did exactly what I swore I wouldn't do," she said, flipping through the pages absently. "I gave her what she wanted."

She snapped the book closed and looked at Peter, a

twinkle in her eye. "But then again, we are fooling her. So I guess I'm *not* doing what she wanted. You're right," at least for now, the shop will stay open until I can figure out a way to save it."

She paused, and cocked her head to one side. "All right, I guess we have no other choice but to go ahead with this charade."

Peter breathed a sigh of relief. "Good, because I can't imagine what your mother might do if you told her the truth."

Alex rolled her eyes and then nodded in agreement.

"We're going to have to get together and sort through the details, but right now I have to meet Claire, to hear her plan for saving the store. I'm starting to feel like some sort of secret agent!" She looked frazzled, but something in her face had softened, some of the stress had disappeared.

Peter looked at her. She was so beautiful, not like Ashleigh, or any of the other polished women at the club. She was unique. She had spunk, and he knew he had to figure out a way to make this charade real.

Chapter Ten

Alex paused in front of Correspondence to catch her breath. She had practically run from her bizarre lunch to the shop, and she wasn't sure what had her more worked up—her mother or the thing with Peter. Maybe it was just Peter in general. What had come over her, agreeing to the charade with him? He must think she was a special kind of crazy, what with all the falling and now this.

She didn't have time to think about that, or about what this would mean for her and Peter. She was about to find out what Claire had come up with. It had to be the answer to her prayers.

She pulled open the glass door, and immediately felt her stress level fall. Her shop felt like coming home every time she walked in. The warm yellow of the walls, the display tables that went down the center aisle—everything about it was warm and welcoming.

A honeysuckle candle filled the entire space with a scent that was sweet yet not overpowering. It sat on the desk where Claire worked with a customer, since the Valentine materials still covered the back table. Claire looked up as she entered, and smiled at her reassuringly. Alex felt herself relax a little bit more. Whatever the plan was, it would work. That was what Claire's smile told her, and that's what she had to believe.

She walked to the back room. Passed the Valentine table, where three college girls sat in their sorority sweatshirts, giggling as they cut and pasted construction paper and hearts together. She stepped through the curtain, took off her coat, and set down her portfolio.

Peter's face flashed in her mind. Why couldn't she stop thinking about him, and why in the world had he been at the East Bank Club? Not that she could be very annoyed—after all, his presence had saved her behind.

It just seemed odd that he had been there in the first place, and it hadn't occurred to her at the time to ask him. She'd been too busy freaking out over what had happened to have any kind of rational thought. That behavior was really going to get her into trouble someday.

The sound of the bells on the front door interrupted her thoughts. Claire must be done with her customer. Time to hear the plan, but as she pulled the curtain from the back room open, she was surprised to see Stephen, smiling ear-to-ear and walking toward her.

"I have good news!" he exclaimed, ushering her into the back room.

"I hope so; you won't believe what I've gotten myself into with my mother now." She rubbed at the crease between her eyebrows, trying to erase the look on her mother's face when she'd met Peter.

"Well, I took the liberty of calling your landlord this

morning to try and renegotiate your lease, and guess what?"

"Stephen, if I wanted to play games, I'd go to one of Claire's game nights and play Guesstures! Please, I can't take anymore—what is the news?"

Stephen stared back at her with wide eyes, and the curtain parted. A stern Claire appeared, and pressed her finger to her lips. "Shh!"

"Sorry," Alex whispered as Claire disappeared behind the curtain again. She turned her frazzled gaze on Stephen, who continued.

"Well, you were right about one thing—Mr. Thompson isn't interested in renegotiating your lease. But that doesn't matter, since he didn't answer the phone, his wife did. And she has recently discovered two things." He paused and Alex glared at him, flapping her hands in hope of getting him to the point.

"One, the building is in her name, and two, Mr. Thompson is having an affair. She very much wants to teach him a lesson, so she's willing to sell the building pretty cheap."

Alex's jaw dropped. There was hope—not for her belief in marriage, but for her shop. She jumped up and pulled Stephen into a hug.

"You did it! You solved my problems."

"Not quite. You still have to get a loan and come up with the money for a down payment. Looking at your books, you shouldn't have any trouble getting the loan, but you need to get the cash together quick, before your father finds out that the building is for sale. If he does, he could start a bidding war."

"Right." Alex felt the hope drain out of her. "Where am I going to come up with that kind of money?"

The bells on the front door jingled again. Stephen shrugged. "At least it's a start. I gotta run. I'll call you later about the loan." And like that he was gone, leaving Alex tangled in the loose ends of her current problems.

"Alex! Are you ready to hear the plan that's going to save this little corner of heaven called Correspondence?" Claire called from the front. Her enthusiasm gave Alex hope, and she hurried to where Claire sat at the front of the shop.

"I hope you're right. Stephen's come up with a way for me to buy the building, but I need cash. Plus, if I don't get the money, based on what I did at lunch today, not only will I lose the shop, but my mother will probably have me committed." Alex sat down across the desk from Claire and prepared for the presentation.

"Well, it all started when I saw this today," Claire began, holding up a full-page ad for the Chicago Bridal Fair. "It was like a light from above shined down on me right there at the Java Bean, and I heard a voice, like in that baseball movie—'if you create them, they will come.' "

Alex knew at that moment exactly why she and Claire got along so well. Claire was as insane as she was.

"I hope you have more than that, because based on that little speech, all I'm hoping for is having you for a roommate when we both land in the loony bin."

Claire rolled her eyes. "Of course there's more than that. We have to get you and this place some serious business. Get Correspondence on every wedding planner's speed dial. What better way to do that than to go to the biggest invitation event in the city?"

Alex scanned the ad again. "That would be a great idea, if I could afford to rent one of those booths—

which I can't, according to my accountant." Alex could feel her spirits falling as the speed of her words increased.

"See, that's where the plan is really brilliant. You aren't going to need to rent a space. The only money we'll need is the cost of the tickets to get us in." Claire was beaming at this point, and Alex furrowed her brow at her friend.

"Come again? How does attending the bridal fair get us any business or make us any money? You aren't making any sense, Claire." This plan was apparently so secret that the logic of it was lost on everyone except Claire.

"Relax, will you? If you'd just let me finish, it will all make perfect sense."

"All right, let's hear this plan of yours, straight through, with no dramatic pauses or anything!" Alex sat back down on the chair and waited for whatever Claire would just say next.

Claire laughed. "Well, I can't promise that, I do have a flair for the dramatic! So, where was I?"

"Well, let's see, the light from above, the voices, no need to rent a booth. Hmmm, I'd say you still haven't really started!" Alex couldn't help but laugh at the absurdity of it all.

Claire laid the paper out on the desk and pointed. "It's being held at the Navy Pier Ballroom, that's where the library convention was held last year, remember?"

Alex didn't, but kept her mouth shut, not wanting to distract Claire, hoping that she would actually make some sort of point in the near future.

"I know that place like the back of my hand. I spent twenty-four hours a day there that week, and part of it

I spent hiding from my boss, remember?" She leaned forward, her eyes widening.

It was coming back to Alex, something about Claire losing the notes for her boss's big speech. She nodded in both agreement and encouragement, and Claire continued.

"I spent so much time hiding out, I'm sure I can find us a secluded, out-of-the-way space like a stairwell or a closet or something, where you can show your invitations." Claire was beaming, as if she had just found the cure for cancer or something.

"Won't we get in trouble for that? I mean, part of paying the registration fee is insuring that everyone attending has the same space and rules to follow that you do." Alex was trying hard to see the positives of this situation. "Besides, what kind of impression are we going to make if we are presenting out of some broom closet?"

"Details, details," Claire mumbled to herself, exasperated. "That's the beauty of it. We'll be the only ones that do make an impression, because we'll be so different from everyone else. Plus, once they get a look at the fabulously unique work we do, they won't care if they're meeting us in a dumpster."

Alex almost believed her. She was right about one thing: they did create exquisite things. Maybe this plan had some hope of working.

"How are they going to find us, since we won't be able to tell anyone we're there—you know, since we won't have paid to be there?"

Not surprisingly, Claire was ready with an answer. "I'll direct them to you, work the crowd, and discreetly point them in your direction." She leaned forward. "That's where the secret part of the plan comes in!"

Alex was picturing them both in trench coats and fedoras, talking in code through the door of the janitor's closet. She shook her head at the thought of it. It was a plan, that was for certain. Besides, if they could pull if off, even get a few orders from it, maybe word of mouth would spread about Correspondence. Only good could come of that.

"You have an answer for everything, so how can it go wrong?" Though actually, she could think of a million ways it could go wrong. "My only question is, what if we get caught and they make us pay the registration fee?"

"Well, I guess we just can't get caught then!" Claire shrugged her shoulders. "So, how'd lunch with your mother go?"

"That's it? That's the end of the discussion about your plan?"

"What else is there to discuss?" Claire asked, holding her hands up in mock protest. "It's a good plan. It'll work if we don't get caught, so we won't be caught. Besides, I can't wait to hear how you got out of lunch without a scratch on you."

Alex stood and walked around the desk to straighten the cards on the wall across from them.

"Actually, I came up with my own secret plan," she said over her shoulder as she continued down the row, straightening the cards as she went. She wanted to avoid looking Claire in the eye as she told her.

"I'm intrigued. Do tell." Claire was enjoying this just a little too much, Alex thought.

"Well, as luck would have it, Peter was having lunch at the club, too. When I introduced him to my mother, she jumped to the conclusion that he was my new boyfriend, and I didn't correct her."

Claire let out a squeal that could have broken the glass on the display cabinets, and Alex turned around to face her.

"Claire, it's no big deal . . ." she began, but Claire was already on her feet and around the desk, words pouring out of her like air from a popped balloon.

"Peter, you mean Dr. Perfect Teeth from the Art Gala and then from the date that you won't talk about. The one that has you smiling to yourself when you think no one is looking at you. That Peter?" She stopped inches from Alex's face and tilted her head.

Alex took a step back. "That date was no big deal, Claire. I told you that. We just had a couple of drinks. I wouldn't even call it a date, come to think of it." Remembering it quickened her heart, which she found completely annoying.

"Whatever you say." Claire smiled knowingly. "Why was he there? Did he play along? Holy cow, what did your mom say? She must have flipped over him," she said, her words coming so fast they practically tripped over each other.

Her hands flew around as she spoke, and Alex had a brief sense of déjà vu—was this how she looked when she got on one of her tangents? Completely unattractive, really.

"Well, yes, he did play along, and yes, my mother was gaga over him. She even gave him a real kiss when she left, not just an air one."

Claire raised one eyebrow in shock—Susan Sanders didn't risk messing up her lipstick for just anyone, and Claire knew it.

"So, what was he doing there?"

"You know, I didn't really have time to ask him. So

about this plan of yours, do you think we should make up some new things or just stick with what we've done in the past?" Alex brushed past her and walked to the front window, hoping that Claire would just let the Peter subject drop, which she knew was next to impossible.

"You're going to pretend to be seeing this guy until you have the money?"

"Yeah—he's game, so what can it hurt? I mean, it's the exact opposite of what my mother wants, you know. The perfect man pretending to be my boyfriend . . . she'll be furious when she finds out."

"Alex, how long have we known each other?" Claire asked.

"About two years." Alex exhaled, her warm breath frosting the window with tiny crystals of ice. "What does that have to do with anything?" Alex turned away from the window to face her friend.

"Well, in all that time, I have never, I repeat never, seen you act this way about a man."

Alex waved her off. "What way? Honestly, Claire, you're making too much out of this guy. Is he handsome? Yes. Kind? Yes. Compassionate? Obviously. I mean, he is a doctor after all. Am I attracted to him? Of course, who wouldn't be?

"But you know me, Claire. I don't have time for all that romance stuff." She turned and adjusted the hearts dangling in the front window that were tangled with each other, embarrassed that she had gotten so emotional over it.

"Rationalize it all you want. Just tell me one thing, Miss Independent. While you're busy pretending he's your boyfriend, how are you going to keep yourself from falling in love with him?"

Alex stopped dead in her tracks, because it was the very question that had lingered in the back of her head since she left him.

Chapter Eleven

Across town, Peter wasn't faring much better. It had become clear to him after "pretending" to be Alex's boyfriend at lunch that he wanted nothing more than to make it real. The problem was, of course, Ashleigh, and the effect his breakup with her was going to have on his career.

He stood in front of the closed door of her father's office—his oh-so-important meeting regarding his future. It had crossed his mind on the way over that perhaps Dr. Rogers was going to tell him he wasn't good enough for Ashleigh. Demand Peter end things with her, even. Dr. Rogers had insinuated as much several times since they had begun dating. It gave Peter a small glimmer of hope as he knocked and an authoritative voice beckoned him into the office.

It was amazing, the transformation from stark hospital corridors to the rich wood panels and plush rugs that decorated the office of the chief of staff. Not to mention the focal point of the room—an enormous picture of Ashleigh that hung on the wall directly behind her father's head. It looked down on the two men as Peter sat in the plush green chair across the massive oak desk from her father.

"Dr. Gibson, I have asked you here this afternoon to discuss your future," his deep voice boomed.

He insisted on calling Peter "Dr. Gibson" when they were at the hospital—to keep things professional, he had said. But it always seemed to Peter that he did it merely to keep him in line. His refusal to admit that there was any type of a personal relationship between them.

The irony was that before Peter started seeing Ashleigh, he had been Dr. Rogers's favorite resident. The man never failed to praise his work or hold him up as an example to the other residents. It had been flattering that someone of such rank had taken an interest in him, and Peter withstood the snickering behind his back from his fellow residents. All that ended the first time Ashleigh had brought him to the club for dinner. The next day Dr. Rogers had moved on to Michael Thompson as his new protégé, riding Peter whenever the opportunity presented itself.

"Yes, sir, that's what I understood this meeting to be about. I will complete my second year of residency in March, and am hoping you'll see fit to name me Chief ER resident," Peter stammered. He hated that this was intimidating.

"Yes, I understand your professional hopes perfectly. However, I want a better understanding of your personal hopes. Specifically regarding my daughter." His voice dripped with superiority.

Well, there it was. The question Peter had dreaded.

His faint hope that his boss would order him out of Ashleigh's life was gone. He grasped the arm of the plush chair to steady himself while he tried to collect his thoughts.

"Ashleigh is a wonderful girl," he began, but was quickly cut off.

"She's more than a wonderful girl. I don't need to tell you that we raised her with certain expectations about life. Expectations I'm not sure you will be able to fulfill."

His tone was all business. However, the conversation seemed to be headed in the right direction. Dr. Rogers was right: Peter couldn't live up to any of their expectations, because he didn't want to.

"Well, as you know, I don't come from much. My education is all I have at this point and I don't own that outright. I have an enormous amount of loans to repay and at the moment, getting a staff position has to be my main focus." That was the truth, no spin needed.

Dr. Rogers looked across the desk at him, and Peter thought for a moment that he had hit the nail on the head.

"I always liked you, Peter."

The use of his first name threw him. This was not what he was expecting to happen.

"Thank you, sir," he stammered, unsure what would come next.

"No thanks needed. You are more than competent as a physician. You do lack some social graces, but I'm sure with Ashleigh's help those will come, with time."

Stunned, Peter wasn't sure what to say. Where was he going with this?

"As I said, my focus is more on getting a job . . ."

Dr. Rogers held up his hands to stop him. "Let me

finish. I liked you, professionally, when you started here. You were ready to learn from the minute you walked through that door, both from the senior staff and from your own mistakes. I respected that about you. But as far as my daughter is concerned, I have to say, I never thought you were good enough for her."

Now this is more like it, Peter thought to himself as he sat quietly, afraid anything he might say would steer the conversation in the wrong direction. Dr. Rogers was right. In the world they lived in, he wasn't good enough for Ashleigh.

"But the time comes for every father to take himself out of the equation when it comes to his daughter's love life. And, according to Ashleigh, the time for me is now."

He did not look happy to be saying it, not in the very least. He looked resigned to his new role, but definitely not happy.

"So, with that in mind, I have just one thing to say to you." He stood and walked around the desk toward Peter. Unsure what to do, Peter stood, if for no other reason than to not be looked down upon, literally.

"I am recommending that you be promoted to Chief ER Resident, but with one condition. If you do anything to hurt my Ashleigh, not only will I remove you from the staff here, but I will make sure you can't get a job anywhere in this city. Are we clear?"

He leaned back against his desk, waiting for a response. Peter's pulse beat furiously in his head; he felt hot with a combination of rage and panic. He cleared his throat to speak.

"Crystal, sir."

"Well, then, this meeting is over." Suddenly the icy

tone was gone from his voice. "I assume I will be seeing you for dinner at the club on Saturday?"

"Yes." What else could he say? He was trapped. His shoulders slumped as he turned to walk out of the office.

But Dr. Rogers had one final blow to land. "Peter, I think you and I both know that it is in our best interests that this conversation stays between the two of us. Ashleigh doesn't need to know anything other than that you are being promoted."

Peter simply nodded and turned to leave without thanking his boss for taking the time to meet with him. *That will show him,* he thought sarcastically.

There was no easy way out now. Ending things with Ashleigh would end his career in Chicago. That was the bottom line.

He pushed the button for the elevator and waited. He had no idea what to do next.

"Meeting with your father-in-law?" Michael asked as Peter joined him in the elevator.

"Ha-ha. He's not my father-in-law, Michael. Ashleigh and I are not engaged," he said, annoyed.

"I'm sure that will change soon enough. Man, I wish I'd seen her first. You are one lucky man. A hot chick like that, with a father who can write you a ticket anywhere you want to go."

Peter had had just about all he could take. "I don't want a meal ticket."

"Oh, yeah. Unlike the rest of us, you want to prove yourself. Man, you're a fool. If I were in your shoes, I'd happily sign up for whatever the old man asked and enjoy the good life."

Peter was about to let him have it when the elevator

doors opened and Michael stepped out, waving over his shoulder as he did. The doors closed, leaving Peter to wish the same thing—if only Michael had met Ashleigh first. He wouldn't be having any of these problems.

He grabbed some water and an apple—the safest things in the hospital cafeteria were things that no one had to prepare—and found an empty table back by the window. Although some of the other residents waved him over to join them, he just waved back. He needed to be alone.

Dr. Rogers and Susan Sanders were a matched pair. Both of them used their money and power to make demands they had no business making. It was something Peter had been dealing with his entire life. People with money ran the show, no matter where you lived or what you did. You could be smarter than them, more driven than them, it didn't matter. They could make things happen that were out of the control of regular people.

His plan for working here, gaining experience, and paying off his loans, were the means to an end for him. His goal from the day he started medical school was to open up a small practice. Though he knew it was far off, he held onto his dream, like Alex and her shop. Both of them ran the risk of losing their dreams because they made no sense to the people who had the power to take them away.

It was so darn frustrating. But he felt sorrier for Alex than himself—at least he wasn't related to his tormentor. Though if Ashleigh had her way, he would be, by marriage. He shuddered at the thought of a lifetime of feeling owned. It wouldn't come to that. Peter could get himself out of this; it just wasn't going to be as quickly as he had hoped.

The thing about guys like Peter that the Dr. Rogerses of the world didn't understand was, once they set their goals, they were willing to work hard to achieve them. He was in it for the long haul, no matter what.

If it meant he was going to have to put his feelings for Alex on hold, then he would just have to do it. Though *how* he was going to do it, he wasn't quite sure.

Chapter Twelve

It had been two weeks since the ill-fated lunch with her mother, and Alex had barely noticed the time had passed. She was up to her elbows in work. The bridal show was fast approaching, not to mention Valentine's Day. Something Claire had said stuck in her mind— about creating more buzz for the store—drumming up business. Alex had taken it to heart and put aside her disdain for the holiday.

She greeted the customers with a smile, made small talk with them about what a glorious holiday it was, biting back her usual combination of wit and sarcasm.

It was exhausting, but every night when she closed the doors, she went to work on the wedding and shower invitations she was designing for the bridal show. In her opinion, most of the other invitation stores were going to be showing the basic, classic invitations. Those were fine. Correspondence sold them, too. However, if they were going to have any kind of impact, they needed things that were fresh and original.

They had to make up for the fact that they weren't actually going to have a booth at the show.

Alex and Claire had been spending their evenings experimenting with different fonts and papers, creating what they thought were some stunning invitations. Then they went on to coordinate shower invitations, thank you notes, even place cards and sample menus—the whole package.

It was a lot of work, but Alex pushed on with the hope that it was going to make a difference and she would be able to buy the building and own the shop outright. The thought of that, of owning the shop without anyone holding anything over her . . . she couldn't even imagine how that was going to feel.

Alex had always thought of herself as an independent woman, but the truth of the matter was that her family's money had always been there if she needed it. It had paid for her education, helped her get her first job, bought her apartment, and helped her open Correspondence. If she thought of it that way, she was far from independent, and that needed to change.

She had just closed the door for the night. It was just six, and she probably could have gotten a few more sales out of the people coming off the El. But she just couldn't wait to open the package of homemade paper that had arrived that afternoon. She had requested one with pressed pansies because she was thinking of doing a garden wedding theme. The artisan who made the paper had promised her some spectacular things, and she couldn't wait to see the others.

Carefully, she slit the tape on the box and opened it to see what was inside. Just as she imagined, they were all wonderful—some with leaves, another with grass, one with rose petals. These were going to blow the competition out of the water. The pansies were as beautiful as she remembered, and she pulled out her file of vellum paper and ribbon to see what would match; a layered look.

The phone rang, and she was so deep in concentration that she nearly fell off her chair.

"Correspondence," she said, annoyed at the interruption. It took everything she had to stay so chipper during the day—after hours, she just couldn't keep it up.

"Well, that isn't going to bring people flocking to the store." Claire giggled on the other end of the line.

"I'm hoping to drive them away tonight. I just got the paper in from Thomas, that artist I mentioned. What time are you going to be here?" Claire had been coming in regularly at night. Stephen had taken to showing up, too. Saving the store had become sort of a team effort, though when they were both there, they were easily distracted. They got involved in conversations that left the two of them laughing or high-fiving each other. Alex had to remind them to stay focused sometimes.

"That's why I'm calling. I can't come tonight. One of the night workers called in sick and I have to hang around here until we close. Sorry."

"No need to apologize, Claire. You've done more than your fair share of work around here. Just because I'm obsessed doesn't mean you have to be." Alex ran her fingers over the paper on her desk. She had three shades of purple ribbon laid next to it, trying to match it to the color of the petals.

"I wouldn't say you're obsessed; more like driven. You know I'd be there if I could. This place is a drag at night. Only computer geeks and reference book readers come to a library after dark." Claire laughed at her own joke.

"Well, just be careful getting home that late. It's not the safest area, you know."

"Actually, Stephen said he would be up this way and would wait and make sure I got home."

"Really? What's he doing in that neighborhood?" Alex set the ribbon down. This was getting interesting.

"Not sure, hold on a second." Alex could tell by Claire's voice that she had taken the phone away from her mouth. "Sir, that book must remain on the third floor. No, you can't. Sir, unless you are currently living on the third floor you most definitely cannot take it home with you. Fine, you do that."

Alex laughed. Claire had an answer for everything.

"I'm back, but I have to run. Someone is trying to download gangster rap on the computers. Is it a full moon or something? Don't stay there all night, you hear? I'll call you back if I get bored, which is doubtful." Then she hung up.

Alex hoped she did call back. She wanted to know more about Stephen walking Claire home. The library was nowhere near his apartment, work, or any client he had mentioned. Maybe *she* was the one who was easily distracted when they'd all been working late. Distracted by the work itself and not paying attention to what was going on between her friends.

Well, obviously that wasn't going to happen tonight. She was alone with her new project. Having picked the perfect ribbon and vellum color, she got to work on the verse and font. This was the part she had trouble with, the part that Claire was so good at—the sentiment and all the romance that went with it.

The font was good, the words, so-so. Creating a sample verse was frustrating because working with her clients inspired her, usually. Once she got to know the bride and groom, it was easy to design for them and create what they had in mind.

These samples she was doing for the bridal show weren't meant to set the stage for a real event, and she was having trouble making things up. It'd probably be best if she just worked on the designs and waited for Claire to do the rest.

The phone rang again, and this time she was ready. It had to be Claire; no one else called after hours. Now she could pick her brain about the invites and see what the deal was with Stephen.

"All right, Claire, spill it. What's going on with you and Stephen?" Alex laughed into the phone.

"Really, Alexandria, is that how you run that little shop of yours? Completely unprofessional."

Alex felt her mouth go dry at the sound of her mother's voice on the other end of the line.

"Mother . . . I was expecting Claire," she stammered into the phone, sitting up straighter as if her mother could see that she was slouching.

"I don't know who that is, darling. But never mind about her. I'm calling to tell you that your father and I have Saturday night available to have dinner with you and Peter, your divine doctor."

Her voice was silky smooth as she said Peter's name. Crap, Alex had completely forgotten about him and the whole charade. Willed herself to do it because she couldn't be distracted by the things she was feeling. She couldn't make sense of them.

"Well, I'll have to check and see if he can make

it—" she started, but, not surprisingly, her mother cut her off.

"Nonsense, dear. I'm sure he will make himself available. We'll see you at seven, at the house. And Alexandria, do wear something attractive, you wouldn't want your own mother to put you to shame when you are trying to impress a man. Ta-ta." The line went dead.

Alex leaped to her feet in her deserted shop, propelled by the frustration she always felt after a conversation with her mother, but this one really took the cake.

"Wear something attractive?" She shouted to no one. "Attractive!" That woman has some nerve, summoning her like that and then actually insinuating that Alex wouldn't know what to wear. She had been going to these little dinners her entire life, and she knew what to wear to them. Not to mention that she had managed to attract her imaginary boyfriend wearing exactly what she pleased, with no help from her mother.

"Someone should point that out to her," she muttered to herself as she attempted to calm her frazzled nerves. Breathing helped, and she leaned to inhale the fragrant, soothing candle on her desk. She felt herself relax.

That quickly passed as she thought of Peter. He hadn't called or stopped in since lunch the day they had devised this plan. Maybe he had changed his mind. Then what would she do? Her head swam as the scene played out in her imagination—dinner at her parents', no Peter, and what that would mean to Correspondence.

She had to sit down and put her head between her legs because she was starting to hyperventilate.

"He wouldn't do that to me, he wouldn't do that to me," she chanted, willing herself to believe it. The phone rang again and she fumbled for it, wondering what her mother had forgotten—perhaps the mayor would be joining them or something.

Fortunately, it was Claire, and Alex lost all thoughts of invitations as she filled her friend in on the conversation she had just had with her mother.

"Peter and I will never be able to fool them. We don't know anything about each other. No one is going to believe we're a couple, let alone my mother. Whom, I might add, has some sort of sixth sense about these kinds of things. Not to mention the fact that Peter hasn't even called me. He probably changed his mind about helping me."

"You haven't called him either, Alex. Maybe he's just waiting for you. Do you have his number?" Claire said matter-of-factly.

"Not the point, Claire. Of course I have the number, but he should have called *me* by now, don't you think?" Alex was breathing hard, like she had just run a marathon or something.

"Well, no. This was *your* plan, remember? Let's see, it's Thursday . . . that gives you just one night to get to know everything about each other. It can work, Alex, just call."

"Fine," Alex said, and Claire laughed.

"I suggest you ask him with a little more enthusiasm if you want to get anywhere. Though he has seen your surly side before, and it hasn't scared him off yet."

"How many times do I have to tell you, nothing is going to happen between the two of us? The mere fact that I haven't spoken to him in two weeks should tell you that," Alex exclaimed, exasperated with her friend.

"So you keep saying. Well, you'll know soon enough, what with tomorrow being Val . . ."

But Alex wasn't listening. She was rummaging through her desk, looking for Peter's number. Finally finding the business card, she flipped it over to where he had written his home number. She was annoyed to feel her pulse quicken at the sight of his scribbled handwriting. He really was a doctor, and had the handwriting to prove it.

"Gotta go, Claire. I need to call Peter before I talk myself out of it." She hung up before Claire had a chance to say good-bye.

Quickly, she dialed his number. After two rings, he answered.

"Hello?" His voice was thick, like he was sleeping, and Alex checked her watch. It was only nine o'clock. Did he really go to bed that early? Then she realized he might; the whole doctor thing probably meant he kept odd hours.

"Peter, it's Alex." She said it so quickly, it sounded like one word.

"Alex," he replied, suddenly alert. "Sorry I haven't called you to work out the details of our little plan. The hospital has been just crazy and I've been covering rounds for some buddies of mine. What's up?"

Alex felt relief wash over her. He was still going to help her. She pinched herself for thinking he wouldn't.

"Well, we need to get together, tomorrow night if possible. My parents have summoned us for dinner on Saturday, and we need to get our stories straight." She rushed on. "Like a practice run for the real thing. Can you make it to my place, say around seven?" She hated how desperate she sounded.

"Seven tomorrow and then dinner Saturday? I should be able to make it—the guys at the hospital owe me after all of the shifts I've covered for them in the last two weeks. Let me make some calls, but I'm sure it's fine."

His voice soothed her, and she felt like it really would be fine. The muscles in her neck relaxed. Peter's calm assurance did wonders for her frazzled nerves.

"Ok, just call me at home—you have that number, right? I'm sorry to be such a pain, but I'll never get to sleep if I don't know for sure." She knew she was being ridiculous, but she couldn't help it that she was neurotic on top of everything else.

"I'll do that. I'm sure it will be fine, Alex; we fooled her once. We'll do it again. Funny that it's tomorrow night, though. Talk to you later."

"Thanks, Peter," she said, and hung up the phone. What did he mean, what he said about tomorrow night? Was it some sort of anniversary or something? Had they met a month ago, maybe? She dismissed the thought as she stood to grab her things. There was way too much to think about to dwell on one off-hand remark.

Dinner tomorrow, and wardrobe for Saturday. Her mind was spinning trying to plan everything in her head. Peter's odd comment was erased as she ticked off the details one by one.

Chapter Thirteen

Bundled from head to toe in practically everything she owned for winter weather, Alex trudged along the un-shoveled sidewalks toward Correspondence. A blizzard was barreling down on the city; snow fell in blankets from the sky, only to be blown this way and that by a bitter, blustery wind—the kind of wind that blew right through a person, the kind of cold that made the inside of her nostrils freeze.

She had overslept, courtesy of staying up too late the night before. Preparing Peter for dinner with her parents was going to be a lot of work. She had to be sure all the bases were covered. Everything from where he grew up to his favorite color to the story about how they met. Her mother would frown upon the scene she had made the night she met Peter. Unfortunately, there were so many other things to learn, Alex didn't think it would be a good idea to make up a story of how they met, too.

She'd woken up late, surrounded by her lists, having

slept through her alarm. Rushing to get ready, she stopped short at her window when she saw all of the snow. Great, now she was going to have to shovel in front of the shop.

It had been a very mild winter so far and Stephen had suggested she cancel the snow removal service to help tighten the expenses of the shop.

"Darn it!" If it wasn't one thing it was another, and her already foul mood had turned darker.

She ended up borrowing a shovel from the storage closet in the basement of her building. It had seen better days, but hopefully it would clear a path to the street, at the very least. Judging from the wind, no shoveled path would stay clear for very long.

Head down, she moved along, her bag over one shoulder, shovel in hand, too preoccupied by her life to really be bothered by the weather. It felt like she was missing something, forgetting something, and it was driving her crazy.

"School, funny childhood stories, politics, no, we should stay away from that—have to remind Peter not to bring up the hospital auxiliary, Mother can't stand the chief of staff's wife . . ." her voice trailed off in the wind. Anyone she passed would think she had lost her mind, which at this point, Alex was starting to think she had.

She reached the door to the shop and was surprised to see a small crowd of people waiting in front. Setting the shovel down and pulling off her gloves to rummage for the key in her bag, she elbowed her way to the front of the crowd. It was only twenty after, not that late. Why in the world would these people wait here, in a blizzard no less? Then it hit her, and she smiled with pride—word was spreading about the shop.

All good feelings came to an end when she heard someone mutter, "It's about time. I bet no one had to wait for Hallmark to open up."

She turned on her heel and was about to declare they could all just march themselves right down the street to Hallmark or Discount Cards or grab one of the bent cards off the rack at the train station when help arrived.

Claire was pushing her way to the front, wearing a bright red stocking hat that hung down to her shoulder with a big pompom on the end, making her look like some sort of elf. She was beaming from ear to ear, and the whole effect, while peculiar, was enough to stun Alex into silence.

"Well, here she is! Now we can all get in and get on with this glorious day." She took the shovel that Alex was holding, wielding at this point, really, and nudged her to find the keys and open the place up. Alex did, and with a bit of a push from the crowd, they all found themselves in the dark but warm shop.

Alex covered the distance to the back room in an instant and turned on the lights and music that always played. She returned to the front, past the group of women who'd settled themselves quickly at the back table, past the men who were jockeying for position in front of the Valentine's display. She stopped at the front desk, where Claire already sat, having removed her enormous parka and hat to reveal an equally festive red sweater. Alex set her bag behind the desk. She looked around the shop, and, seeing the smiling faces of the customers, felt herself relax a bit.

"How about I stay here and work the crowd and you go out and work on the sidewalk?" Claire offered as she settled back into the chair.

"That is exactly what I was thinking," Alex said as she rifled through the folders that lay in a neat stack at the side of the desk. "If you get a minute, why don't you take a look at the things I did last night?"

"Love to!" Claire practically erupted, and Alex looked at her friend, mystified by her enthusiasm.

"All right, I know I've been wrapped up in the ongoing saga of my life. Obviously, I have missed something where you are concerned. Are you going to share?"

Claire smiled sheepishly at her, and then began sifting through the folders Alex had put before her. "Nothing really to share," she replied off-handedly.

"Claire, you're beaming. Something is certainly going on. If I weren't sure I was going to get a fine from the city for all that snow out front, I would stay here and badger you until you fessed up. So, I suggest you either tell me now, or accept the fact that one way or another, I will get it out of you when I am done!"

Claire ignored her and turned to the man who had joined them with a card in his hand, ready to pay.

Alex stepped back out into the blustery day. She wasn't going to get anywhere with Claire, anyway. Surveying the sidewalk, she pulled her scarf tighter around her face and dug into the mountains of snow that piled around her, glad to have something to put her energy into and distract her from her crazy life for a moment.

She had never actually shoveled anything, having grown up in a home that hired people to do that sort of thing. How hard could it really be?

Two hours later, her arms and back aching, she was fully aware of exactly how hard it was. In movies or on the news, it seemed as though people just effortlessly plunged their shovels into the piles of snow and just as easily dumped them somewhere else. Breathing heavily, she leaned against the front window and looked at her work with no satisfaction.

The sidewalk peeked through in small patches; packed snow had impeded her progress. She literally ran into at least twenty people, so intent on her job, so lost in her own thoughts. Most of them had just muttered a "pardon me," though others had cursed at her. If her mouth hadn't been buried beneath her scarf, she would have had something to say back to them.

Through the window, inside the cozy shop, Alex watched Claire sit at the desk, a line of customers stretching almost to the back table. It had been like that for most of the morning, and though her whole, frozen body ached, Alex was glad to have a break from all those people and their romantic entanglements.

"Nice work! See, you didn't really need that snow removal service." Stephen's voice pulled her from her thoughts.

He held a tall paper cup towards her, steam streaming from the small hole on the top. She took it eagerly and drank, the hot liquid warming her inside, but not out.

"I wouldn't go that far. What is this, the blizzard of the decade?" She shook her head in disbelief.

"Actually, they're calling it the storm of the century on the radio. We're supposed to get almost two feet before it gives up." He nodded toward the shop. "Things look to be going well in there." His eyes focused on where Claire sat, and something in Alex's mind clicked.

"Stephen! You and Claire, that's what she's smiling about." She stabbed a mittened finger into his chest. "Why you're going to the library at night. How long has this been going on?" She slugged her friend playfully on the arm and he blushed.

"Not long. I mean, nothing's going on. We're just hanging out," he stammered, his eyes never leaving the scene inside the shop. Claire, with a break in her sales, glanced up and saw Stephen through the window. The smile on her face told Alex something different.

"I have some new numbers for you, projections for the bridal show. If you have time, I thought we could go over them. Lunch, perhaps?" His voice was all business suddenly, trying to distract Alex from prying any farther.

A snowplow barreled by loudly and Alex had to shout over it to be heard.

"Sure, just let me check with Claire and see if she has anywhere to be." She leaned the shovel against the doorframe and stuck her head in, not wanting the snow on her boots to mess up the floor. Next, Stephen's budget would have her cleaning her own carpets.

The thought of using one of those Rug Doctor machines she saw at the grocery store distracted her momentarily. Then a gaggle of girls making their way out of the store with homemade cards held tightly in their hands flustered her even more.

A cold wind blew through the open door and Claire looked at her intently.

"If you have this under control, Stephen wants to go over some numbers with me." Alex called out. "I'll bring you back some lunch?"

Claire waved her off. "You'll need your strength; the snow isn't letting up much." She glanced at the window where Stephen stood. "Soup, you can bring me some soup. And don't hurry back—it's all under control."

Alex joined Stephen back outside and the two of them headed off for lunch, bracing themselves against the wind that blew snow at them from every direction. They stopped at the first restaurant they came to and went inside.

"Let's go to the back, away from the draft," Stephen suggested, and she followed his lead to a table near the kitchen where it was considerably warmer. She took off her various outerwear—hat, scarf, mittens, finally her coat, and then took her seat.

"Please tell me you have some good news," she said as he took his seat across the small square table, having gone through the same routine of disrobing.

"Well, not great news, but good, I think." He pulled a file from his briefcase and set in front of her. "I looked at your inventory. Your orders pending as well as the merchandise you have ordered for next season. Your sales are up this month compared to last year, but that isn't enough to earn you what you need." He pointed to a graph on the second page that apparently told her what she needed to accomplish. "You really need to get some big sales at this bridal fair thing."

The waitress appeared and quickly took their order. Stephen continued.

"So, from what Claire says, you have some great things for the show. If it all goes as planned, you should be fine. Next month at this time, we'll be celebrating your independence. Unless, of course, you and the good doctor turn out to be for real." He shuffled the papers and put them back into the file folder, then continued. "That's what Claire thinks is going to happen, by the way."

"All right, if you aren't going to admit something is going on between the two of you, then you have to stop with all this 'Claire says' stuff." She smiled across the table as his cheeks, already red from the cold, turned a shade of crimson.

She continued. "The whole Peter thing is what it is, nothing more. You know me, Stephen. I try to steer clear of all that drama. It's just not me. It never works out." She took a drink of her coffee and stared at him across the table.

He shook his head. "Alex, I think that you really believe that. To be honest, I believed it, too." He leaned forward. "But here's the thing I've figured out: that's only right if you're with the wrong person." He paused and looked at Alex, who shifted uncomfortably in her seat.

"If you find the *right* person, then you can just be yourself. All that crap we hate about relationships, none of it happens. It's just like hanging out with a friend, except so much better. That's all I'm going to say about it."

He picked up his spoon and dipped it into his soup. Not knowing what else to do, Alex did the same. They ate without saying another word. The noise from the people in the restaurant became the background to their silent difference of opinion, until they were both finished eating.

The waitress appeared with their check and a brown bag containing Claire's lunch.

"You ready to head back?" Stephen said, breaking the silence as he stood to bundle up again.

"Actually, no. I think the shop will do much better if I leave Claire in charge for as long as possible today. I'm going to finish my coffee and look at these numbers. Tell her I'll be back soon."

Stephen pulled on his coat and grabbed the check and the paper bag on the table.

"Unless you give it a chance, you'll never know, Alex. Maybe things could be great with Peter, and maybe not, but Claire and I both think we've never seen you act this way, about anyone." He looked at her sincerely. "And that has to mean something."

"I thought you weren't going to say anything else," she teased, relieved that the tension of their lunch was gone.

"I meant about me and Claire," he clarified. "Your love life is fair game, as far as I'm concerned." He winked and patted her on the head with his mittened hand. Then turned and walked toward the steamy windows in the front, pausing at the register to pay. He waved to her before he pushed the door open and stepped out into the storm, leaving her with so much on her mind, she didn't know where to begin.

The columns of numbers in front of her blurred and she closed the file and pushed it aside. She took a sip of coffee, her fingers curling around the mug, still cold from her morning's work.

Claire and Stephen. She hadn't seen that coming. No two people deserved happiness more, and if they found it together, then she couldn't be more pleased for them.

Maybe Stephen was right about finding the right person. After all, he and Claire practically glowed with happiness. She thought about the time she had spent with Peter, how it made her feel and how easy it was to be in his company.

Her stomach fluttered as anxiety made its way up her arms. It was her natural reaction to the thought of relationships. She looked at the file on the table and opened it back up to look at the numbers, determined to make sense of them.

No, she wouldn't be distracted by all Stephen's talk of love. Raising the money for the down payment was all she could think about.

Relationships were fine for other people. Not for her, no matter how great it had felt that night to kiss Peter.

"Aghhh!" she said aloud, and then was embarrassed to find everyone at the surrounding tables staring at her. It was too much for one woman to deal with—the shop, her parents, love and relationships as a whole, and what in the world had she forgotten?

That nagging feeling she had started the day with was still there. That alone was enough to drive her crazy, not to mention the image in her mind of Peter's smile, surrounded by the rest of his perfectness.

Chapter Fourteen

There was a note taped to the door of her apartment asking if she knew anything about a missing shovel when Alex blew in from what had been one of the longest days of her life.

She had sat at the diner and gone over the numbers from Stephen time after time, her mind unable to focus on them. Finally, she gave up and went back to the shop.

The sidewalk was completely covered with snow again when she returned. Then in the midst of re-shoveling, a delivery truck containing a good portion of her stock for spring slid to a stop in front of her. The alley where she normally took deliveries was blocked with snow, so the deliveryman carried box after box through the front door, a trail of dirty snow and slush from there to the back room marking his path.

When it began to be obvious that the snow was not going to let up, she conceded her defeat and spent the remainder of the day cleaning the carpet and checking

the order in. Claire remained happily at the desk, helping person after person. Finally the clock turned five,
and they were able to close the doors and head out into
the frigid air of the raging blizzard.

"Thanks for all your help today. As crazy as it was, I
would have lost it without your help, I'm sure," Alex
told her friend as she pulled the door closed to lock up
for the day. Her arms and back ached from all the shov-
eling. All she wanted to do was crawl into a hot bubble
bath and put this day behind her.

"Well, it's all over now and tomorrow things will get
back to normal," Claire said, pulling on the horrible hat
she had worn that morning.

"Normal, yeah, whatever that is anymore." Alex
chuckled. "Listen, Claire, I know you don't want to talk
about it, but I am really happy for you and Stephen."

"Thanks," Claire turned, her face practically glowing. "It's just so new, and so good. I don't want to jinx
it. Have a good time tonight."

Alex felt her pulse quicken. Tonight. Peter. While
she'd been running from one thing to the next, she had
managed to forget her plans for the evening completely. There would be no soothing bath for her. Nope, the
saga of her life spun on.

"You do the same," she said quickly. "I have to get
home." Visions of her messy apartment flashed through
her mind and she waved to Claire as she turned to walk
toward the El. Claire went the opposite way, toward
Stephen's office, Alex noted. Walking as quickly as the
weather would allow, she headed home, her mind spinning as usual.

Pulling the note off the door as she pushed it open
with her shoulder, she made a mental note to bring the

shovel home with her tomorrow. She'd have to come up with something to make it up to her Super, wine perhaps. If they didn't drink it all tonight, that is.

She busied herself cleaning up, straightening things in her usually tidy apartment. It was easier to straighten than to think about what Stephen had said to her.

What if he was right? She couldn't seem to shake off the nagging question. What if all the things she hated about a relationship—the games and insecurities—just weren't the case if you found the right person? What if the right person for her was Peter?

It couldn't be. She tried to reassure herself. He wasn't interested in her that way. Was he? As far as she could tell, she was some sort of pet project to him—a distraction from his serious life as a doctor.

First with the ankle and then with this plan to fool her mother—it was just entertainment for him, that had to be it. He must feel sorry for her or something. Who wouldn't, really? Based on their shared experiences, he must think she was a lunatic. He was trying to save her from herself or something like that. Though it irritated her to no end, it did seem that every time he showed up, she needed a white knight.

She pulled out wine glasses and poured the chips she had bought into a basket. Placing it all on a tray and carrying it to the now clean coffee table in her living room, she stepped back to look at the scene. Her eyes stopped on the candles arranged next to the tray.

If she lit them, what kind of message would it send? A warm, welcoming look was what she was going for. Not a romantic one. If Claire were coming over, she would light them. Stephen, too, she reasoned as she struck the match and held it to the wick.

Just as they lit, the CD playing softly in the background changed to a slow, romantic song. Her stomach clenched. In a panic, she blew them out. She didn't want to give him the wrong idea.

Or did she? Didn't the white knight deserve some making out on the sofa?

More wine. That was the answer. She'd get another bottle for her Super for the shovel, or maybe make him cookies or something. She was definitely going to need something to help her relax. Apparently, it was going to be wine. Checking her watch, she panicked when she saw how little time she had to get herself ready. Hopefully the storm would make him late.

She worried that her cheeks, still bright red from the icy wind, would stay that way permanently, as she powdered them down in front of the mirror in the bathroom. When that didn't help, she applied a lip gloss in a complementary color. Her hair was a mess from spending most of the day shoved under a hat, but she twisted it up in her usual clip. Aside from the unruly pieces that refused to be tamed, it did look better.

She took one last look in the mirror. She was presentable, which was the best she could do tonight. She checked her watch. Five after six. The storm was slowing him down, so there was probably time for another glass of wine.

As she poured it, a picture of him, fighting the storm on a big white horse enroute to her apartment, conjured itself up in her mind. Her white knight, riding to her rescue, once again annoyed Alex.

A knock at the door interrupted her thoughts. She took a swallow from the glass and took a deep breath. *Here goes nothing,* she thought, as she crossed the room to let him in, wishing she had lit the candles after all.

Peter inhaled sharply as the door swung open and he got a look at Alex. Standing there in the doorway, her lips slightly glossed, her cheeks full of color, and her hair slightly unkempt, she was the most perfect woman he had ever laid eyes on. His self-imposed break from her the last two weeks had done nothing to lessen his burgeoning feelings.

Now here she was right in front of him, and all he wanted was to pull her into his arms and kiss her like she had kissed him that first night. But in the back of his head, the ever-present voice of good conscience reminded him to remember Ashleigh. So instead, he simply said hello as she motioned him through the door and into her apartment.

"Sorry I'm late. The snow is really coming down still." Bending over, he pulled his boots from his feet, placing them on a blue rug next to Alex's, and then he took off his coat and looked around for a place to put it.

"Let me take that," she said, sticking her arms out to take it from him. "Pour yourself some wine and settle in. We have a lot of work to do," she called over her shoulder as she disappeared into what appeared to be the bedroom with his coat.

Business. Yes, he would simply look at this whole evening like a study session. Maybe that would help him stay focused, but it was doubtful. Alex didn't look like any med student he had come across. A bottle of red wine sat on a marble coaster on the table in front of him, and he poured a glass.

"So, I made some lists of things we need to know

about each other to pull this off." Alex reappeared from the bedroom with some sort of clipboard. "You know, couple-like things."

He swallowed hard on his wine. "Couple-things? Like what?"

She crossed the room and sat down on the other end of the couch, reaching for her glass of wine.

"Just some of the basics: childhood stories, favorite colors, things we like to do together, that sort of thing." She lifted her glass to her lips and shuddered. "Is it cold in here?"

"No, I think it's fine. So what do you want to know first, my childhood stories or my favorite color? Let's save shared interests for last." He said it with an unintended hint of flirtation. His cheeks flushed.

"In his infinite wisdom, my friend Stephen somehow managed to convince me I didn't need snow removal for the remainder of the winter. Cost-cutting measures, which is great, until you have to shovel two feet of snow. Can you hand me that blanket?"

Her endless streams of dialogue never ceased to amaze him. He had never met anyone who used so many words.

She pointed to a green chenille throw draped along the couch behind him. Peter reached around and grasped the soft fabric between his fingers. Then he stood in a grand dramatic gesture to cover her with it, but as he flung the blanket out, he knocked his wine glass over. Wine splashed out in a great arc, sending drops of red everywhere on the table and inching its way towards the carpet.

Alex jumped up and ran toward the kitchen. Returning with a roll of paper towels, she dropped to her knees and tended to the spill. As Peter tried to get out of her way, his feet got tangled in the blanket he still held and he fell onto the couch, inches from knocking her glass off the table next to him. However, he didn't miss the basket of chips, which went flying all over Alex.

"God, I'm sorry, Alex," he said as he thrashed around trying to untangle himself from the blanket. "I was just trying to be funny, you know, with the blanket."

She looked up at him, and when he emerged from the blanket, their eyes met and both of them burst into laughter.

"I didn't realize clumsiness was contagious." She laughed, picking chips off her lap.

"I don't remember learning that in med school, but maybe you have a rare form that is easily transmitted." He laughed, pulling some paper towels from the roll beside her and pressing them into the carpet.

"Salt will take this up," he said with authority. "Do you have some?"

"Salt? Yes, I have some. How in the world do you know that?" she asked as she stood, trying as she did to catch the chips that fell from her lap.

"My mom had a remedy for everything. Every spot, stain, or malady—she knew some way to fix it." He stopped blotting up the wine as Alex returned and handed him the salt. He sprinkled the stain generously, then handed the box back to her.

"There. Now we just let it sit for awhile and then vacuum it up." He turned to find that she had walked back into the kitchen, returning without the salt but with more chips, which she poured into the now empty basket.

Not knowing what to do, he sat back down and poured himself another glass of wine.

Turning to face her, he burst out laughing.

"What?" she asked, confusion on her face.

He reached forward to pluck a chip from her hair and handed it to her. She laughed herself as she took it from him, and as their fingers touched, the room went dark.

"I wondered how long the power would hold with this wind," she murmured. "Stay put while I light some candles. We don't want you to fall and hurt yourself," she teased.

It was pitch black, and he felt her walk past him and heard her rustling around for what he assumed to be matches. Striking one, she held it to the candles that sat on the table in front of them, her face glowing above them.

"Good thing these weren't lit before or my whole apartment might have caught fire." She giggled.

"It wasn't that bad of a fall," he protested, joining in her laughter.

Then something occurred to him.

"Well, this is turning out to be a picture-perfect Valentine's Day."

"What did you say?" Her shock registered in her voice and on her face.

"You know—a perfect Valentine's day—wine, candles. All we're missing is chocolates and, well, romance, I guess." He turned to face her and laughed as she sat speechless beside him. "Don't tell me you forgot. Isn't this kind of a big day in your line of work?"

From the expression on her face, he could tell she had forgotten. And darn if the bewilderment he saw there wasn't just as beautiful as every other expression that crossed her face, especially in the candlelight.

Chapter Fifteen

"Valentine's Day?" she murmured, her brow creased with confusion. Then, like a slideshow, images flashed in her mind: Claire in her hat. The red sweater she was wearing. All those people lined up in front of the store in the middle of the blizzard. All the comments about how after today, things would be different. It all made sense, and she couldn't believe she had missed the signs. Not to mention the fact that it was as simple as looking at a calendar.

She jumped up and paced around the room, her hands flying this way and that. She couldn't possibly sort it all out while she was still.

"I can't believe I forgot it was Valentine's Day," she rambled on. "I mean, you're right, it *is* a big day for my line of work, and I completely forgot it. What's wrong with me? I think I actually might be cracking up here." She stopped and looked at Peter, where he sat very still on the couch, almost as if he was afraid to move.

Then, slowly, a smile crossed his face, which was a mistake because it just added fuel to her fire.

"You think this is funny? I swear, it's like suddenly I'm living someone else's life—a *pretend* date with a *pretend* boyfriend on Valentine's Day, of all days." Her voice reached a fevered pitch as she stopped her pacing and stood directly in front of him, wanting to make her point as clearly as she could.

"So that distraction, the work involved in pulling off this giant farce, makes me forget one of the biggest days of the year for the very thing I'm doing all of this to save. It's insane, I'm insane!" she ended matter-of-factly as she flopped down next to him on the couch and downed the remainder of her wine.

"Can I get you a little more?" he asked, reaching for the bottle.

Alex nodded and held her glass out to him. Silence filled the dim room, shadows stretching to the edge of the circle of light created by the candles.

"If you want to go, I'd understand. I mean, how much crazy did you sign on for, really?" She laughed to herself as she tilted her head and rested it on the back of the couch, closing her eyes.

"I knew," Peter said cautiously.

"Knew what?" She turned her head and looked at him, confused.

"That it's Valentine's Day," he said slowly, all hints of sarcasm gone from his voice. "I wanted to come here tonight—so maybe I'm the crazy one."

Alex's stomach fluttered, which she found both exciting and annoying. He knew it was Valentine's Day. He wanted to be here, with her. What did that mean? Her mind spun with the possibilities. Peter wanted to help her, and maybe he felt sorry for her—or maybe he wanted her.

That last possibility caused her to clamp her eyes shut again and roll her head to face the wall on the other side of the couch. Lost in a mental picture that she was embarrassed by, his voice snapped her back to reality.

"I'm not leaving; we have a, what did you call it? A 'pretend' relationship to plot and a shop to save. Isn't that right?" Peter chuckled beside her.

It was the answer she should have wanted, but for some reason, it left her feeling a bit disappointed. She was wearing lip gloss, after all. Didn't he see that?

She shook her head in disbelief. "I don't get it. Why in the world would you do that? What do you get out of this?"

"I have never met anyone like you," he said with sincerity. "Every time we're together, I find myself wondering what will happen next. I like you, simple as that. And there's the fact that you or those around you could probably benefit from having a trained medical professional near them at all times." His blue eyes sparkled in the candlelight.

They both laughed. Though Alex still felt like she was losing her grip on things, the panic about it subsided. She took a deep breath and reached for her clipboard.

"Well then." She turned to face him, curling her feet up under her on the couch. "What's your favorite color?"

They spent the rest of the evening shooting questions back and forth at each other, listening to each other's answers about their likes and dislikes. One by one, Alex checked things off her list until eventually, they didn't need it anymore. Somehow, they found themselves in a genuine conversation.

"So, you're a small town boy, huh?" she inquired. "It must have been hard for you here at first."

"It was a bit of culture shock, say the least." He smiled. "The hardest part for me was how unattached everyone seemed to be. I remember going to the grocery store with this buddy of mine, and I kept saying hello to everyone and no one responded. I was really starting to get irritated about it, and finally he tells me that you just don't do that here. And I said, 'you mean, be friendly?' He just shrugged his shoulders at me. I couldn't believe it." Peter shook his head.

"But it didn't stop you," Alex retorted.

"What do you mean?"

"The night we met, people weren't exactly rushing to my aid." She smiled at him. "And I wasn't all that friendly when you tried to help me."

"You were just embarrassed. Though, now that I've spent some time with you, I have to wonder why. You must be used to causing a scene by now."

Alex punched him playfully on the arm in mock protest. Unfortunately, he was right. She was used to it.

"I'm not the one who spilled a full glass of wine tonight, though, am I?" She laughed. "Speaking of which, do we need to open another bottle?" She pointed to the now-empty one that sat in front of them.

"I'd love to, but I have the early shift tomorrow. I traded with someone so that I could make our big dinner tomorrow night. I'd take some water, though." He got up from the couch and walked into the kitchen. "Just tell me where the glasses are."

"In the cupboard to the right of the sink. Grab me one, too, with lots of ice." Alex set her empty wine glass on the coffee table. Water was a good idea; her head was spinning a little from the wine.

Peter returned carrying the two glasses, one of which he handed to her as he sat back down on the couch. "So, enough about me," he said his voice rich in sarcasm. "Tell me about you."

"What do you want to know?" Alex replied in the same tone.

"Well for starters, why does a woman like you need a pretend boyfriend?" He grabbed a handful of chips and stared intently at her, waiting for an answer.

Alex felt a subtle change in the tone of their conversation, and whether it was the lack of heat in the apartment or the question itself, a chill ran through her and she shivered.

"Boy, it doesn't take long for it to get cold in here once the heat goes off, does it?" She skirted the question, but Peter wasn't going to let her get away with it.

"Answer the question, please. I need to know so I can tell your parents how I managed to change your mind," he prodded.

Alex swallowed hard. "I have a hard time with that relationship stuff," she said matter-of-factly. After all, it was the truth.

"Why?" He shivered, too, reassuring her that it was the chill in the room. She held a corner of the blanket that covered her out to him and he slid over, closer to her, and pulled the blanket around himself. The heat of his body made her ask herself the same question.

"Well, for starters, you've met both my parents, but you haven't seen anything yet. Wait until tomorrow night when they're together. They make even the most dysfunctional relationship seem good." She was sitting in the corner of the couch facing Peter. Looking at him, she was struck again by how handsome he was.

"So, bad role models, huh?" He turned his head and looked at her.

She shrugged. "My parents, though married, operate as independent beings. They seem to have no use for each other, unless it's to manipulate the other one. When I was little, it wasn't as bad. My dad was actually pretty fun, but little by little he became someone else. Maybe it's a cop-out, but I just always blamed it on my mother and her forcing him to be someone he wasn't."

"So you think that if you fall for someone you'll lose yourself?" Peter asked, his voice soft and caring, as if he wanted to get to the root of her problems.

Alex nodded. It was the truth—one she had lived with and observed in everyone she knew, with the exception of Claire and Stephen. But then again, they were just starting out, so who knew what would happen with them?

She had never shared that with anyone before. With everyone else, she had just used the whole "independent woman too busy with her life to be concerned with a man" thing. It was strange how freeing it was to have shared her most personal thoughts with Peter. Usually opening up to anyone made her hostile, but not tonight.

"What about you? My mother will be dying to know how someone like you managed to stay unattached for so long." Suddenly, so was Alex. Thoughts of Peter being too good to be true flashed in her mind.

"Too busy, I guess. I'm just focused on my goal," he

said quickly. "Nice change of subject, though. Would you rather tell me about your favorite color?"

Alex blushed. "Green. My favorite color is any shade of green."

The conversation continued, though Alex did her best to steer clear of the serious subjects. And as the candles burned low and the wind outside howled, she was amazed to find how much they had in common. More and more, she was beginning to think that Peter wasn't too good to be true. He was simply good.

Chapter Sixteen

The phone was ringing as Peter jiggled his key in the lock, but he felt no need to hurry—he already knew who it was. The key finally turned and the old wooden door creaked open. Ashleigh's voice was echoing through the dark, empty space as he made his way into his small studio. He leaned against the wall next to the table where the phone sat and listened.

"Peter, it's Ashleigh. Where could you be?" She paused and Peter could picture her forehead crease as she tried her best to imagine just where he could be.

"Anyway, I am having a marvelous time with Mother here in New York. We have been hitting all the boutiques and getting so many beautiful things. Don't worry, I haven't forgotten you while I'm out shopping. Stefan is everything I imagined and more. I stopped in at Tiffany's to see if they have a good selection, and of course they do, so that might have to be a possibility." She giggled in what he knew she thought was an endearing way. "So call me when you get this. I just can't imagine where you might be. Bye." Then she hung up.

How like Ashleigh to forget he was supposed to be at work. His job was out of her small universe, aside from the title it could give her. The goal of being a doctor's wife didn't seem to remind her that he worked long hours at the hospital. If he hadn't switched his shift, that's exactly what he would have been doing tonight. He seized at his annoyance with her, happy to be able to focus on something.

Ashleigh had flown to New York with her mother at the last minute, something about being able to get in with Stefan, the new "it" person in the spa world. From what Peter could gather, it was almost like getting an audience with the Pope in Ashleigh's mind. She had called on the way to the airport, hoping he wouldn't mind postponing their Valentine's plans.

Were they even in the same relationship? he wondered, as he often did lately when it came to Ashleigh. Couldn't she see that he wasn't there anymore? He'd been doing his best to put some distance between them. Even if she was missing that key piece of evidence, where did she think the money for an engagement ring would come from at this point in his life, especially one from Tiffany's?

Maybe he should pop the question with the chip of a diamond he could afford from the chain jewelry store at the mall. That would probably send her running for the hills. The thought brought a flicker of hope, but the ridiculousness of it brought him to his senses. She wouldn't run. She'd calmly go to her father and insist he help Peter upgrade to what she wanted. Then he'd be stuck deeper than he was now.

His gaze fell on the silver frame that held her picture on the table next to his bed. When she'd placed it there, he had been crazy about her. Being her pet project hadn't really bothered him. She had a sweetness about her, an innocence from being brought up in a totally protected environment. He had enjoyed being with her—fallen for her giggle and her helplessness. The change in her seemed to happen overnight, this obsession with marriage and the status it would allow her.

It had started innocently enough. After one of the several weddings they had attended last fall. Suddenly it was as if she was the only single woman in the city. It was all she thought or talked about. Planning a wedding was what she lived and breathed for, so much so that she no longer seemed aware he was involved in the relationship with her at all. As annoying as it was, he felt just a little bit sorry for her, too.

Peter moved through the small space and found his way to the bed. There wasn't really room for anything else, as small as it was. He used one of those cardboard dressers for a bedside table, and his desk was an old door he had found in the basement of his building laid across milk crates that held his most important and prized possessions, his medical school textbooks. The look of the place screamed of struggling med student, but he wasn't trying to impress anyone. That was, after all, what he was.

He lay down without turning on the light. The phone call only added to the mixture of emotions he was feeling. Tonight cemented what he already knew—he was falling in love with Alex. There was no way around it, no way to fight it. It was the simple truth, though not one he'd planned on.

Sitting with her tonight under that blanket, it was all he could do to keep from pulling her close to him and kissing her and telling her about it. He had come close, telling her he knew it was Valentine's Day, and letting her know that he had chosen to be there with her. It had been enough tonight.

He groaned and pulled the pillow over his face as he pictured Alex curled up in the corner of the couch. Listening so intently as he told her about how little his family had when he was growing up. Her face turned slightly, candles flickering small shadows across it, one curl of her hair hanging down to the side that she kept trying to tuck back into place. So beautiful, and she didn't even know it.

He had told her things tonight that he had never told anyone. Shared parts of his childhood he usually skimmed over. Embarrassed not because they'd been poor, or because of their lack of material possessions, but by having to listen to his mother apologize for it. That had been the hardest part for him when he was growing up, and Alex had such compassion for that. He could hardly believe that she had grown up wealthy. Then again, she'd lacked what she wanted in her childhood—love and attention from her parents.

It really was remarkable that she had become the person she was—unselfish, and keen to stay out of the limelight. From what he could tell, the only damage done from her childhood was her idea of how horrible relationships were. He could change her mind about that, because he had no interest in changing anything else about her. No, to him Alex Sanders was beyond perfect. But until he and Ashleigh had called things off, he couldn't even entertain the thoughts he was having tonight. Because if he acted on them, it would prove that what Alex thought of men was true. They were liars and cheats. That's what she had said.

Though she was bitter about relationships, it didn't seem to stop her from being a caring person. Her sincere interest in what he was saying was why he'd left so quickly. She had reached over and taken his hand. It was just a friendly, compassionate gesture that to her was the natural thing to do. But to him, the feel of her small soft hand on his had startled him back into the reality of what was going on.

He had almost knocked over the candles as he leaped up, making excuses as he went. He'd confirmed the plans for the big dinner with her parents, all the while pulling on his boots and coat. Hurrying out her front door and into the still stormy night without realizing the boots were on the wrong feet. Not breathing until the frigid night air had forced itself into his lungs.

What was he going to do? It had been enough tonight, but it wouldn't be enough forever. Not to mention the fact that once she had raised the money she needed, she wouldn't need Peter anymore. He sensed she was feeling something for him; there was that kiss, after all. But after tonight, he knew that Alex could easily convince herself it was nothing when their little charade was up. Her parents had really screwed her up in the relationship department, and his current situation left him in no position to change her mind.

Getting Ashleigh to end things was his only way out. But how to do it? He was giving all the signals he could that they weren't in the same place, but it wasn't deterring her.

The strobe light from a passing snowplow lit up the

room, and the scrape of the blade against the street outside as it passed gave an eerie echo of how he felt.

Discouraged further, he crossed the room to put away his coat, flicking on the light in the small hallway to see what he was doing. The power must not have gone out on his side of town, he thought, noticing the message indicator on his answering machine blinking "two." Someone else had called before Ashleigh, and he pushed the play button.

"Peter, buddy, it's Michael. Listen, just wanted to say thanks again for switching shifts with me. Unfortunately, my evening wasn't as productive as I would have liked. Don't get me wrong, I met some lonely ladies without a Valentine, just no one with a pedigree like your little meal ticket. I'll fill you in tomorrow. Thanks again, buddy."

Peter was filled with disdain for Michael. They were friends, but lately all Michael could talk about was hooking up with anyone who had connections. He really got into the whole social scene of being a doctor, and longed to climb the prestigious ladder that had rungs of country clubs and gala charity events—anything that got his name in the paper.

His message ended, and before Peter could push the button to skip it, Ashleigh's message played again. Crossing the room to the refrigerator, he pulled open the fridge and grabbed an apple, miming along with the sickly sweet words that she had recorded earlier.

Then he stopped, frozen by the inspiration that had just struck him. How had he not have seen it when it was right in front of his face? It was like two pieces of a puzzle fitting together. Relief flooded through him at the hint of a solution. Everyone would be happy, everyone would get what they wanted.

Michael and Ashleigh were perfect for one another. Even their names seemed to flow together as he repeated them out loud—"Michael and Ashleigh. Dr. and Mrs. Michael Harris. That's it!"

They wanted exactly what the other had to offer. There would be no guilt on Peter's part for letting Ashleigh down—he'd be giving her the husband she always wanted, just not him. How had he not seen it before now? It was the answer for all of them. He just had to make them see it.

Chapter Seventeen

"Alright, are you ready?" Alex looked at Peter and tried to compose herself. This was it. If she—or they, rather—could pull this off, she could breathe just a little easier. She would have the time she needed to save the shop. But why did she feel like she had stepped right into a bigger mess?

As if to add fuel to the already burning fire, Peter grabbed her hand. Instinctively she tried to shake it off, just as the giant oak door swung open and there stood her parents. Her mother smiling her best welcome-to-my-home socialite smile, her father a few paces behind, a highball full of scotch already halfway empty.

"Darling, come in out of the cold." Susan's tone went through Alex quicker than even the frigid Chicago wind. She stood on the threshold, unable to make herself take the step into the grand entryway, until she felt a slight pressure on her lower back. She turned slightly and caught Peter's reassuring gaze, and then, following his prompt, stepped into the house.

137

"Good evening, Mother. Dad, you remember Peter?" she asked, her voice wavering.

Peter stepped forward, his hand extended toward her father. "Mr. Sanders, nice to see you again."

Her father stuck his hand out and met his grasp. "Yes, Dr. Gibson, isn't it? You look different standing up, and not on top of Alex." He chuckled to himself and Alex shot him a dirty look. She was going to have to get him alone later and let him have it. After all, he had encouraged her to pursue Peter, and that was what she had done, as far as her father knew. Poor Peter was going to get both her parents at their very worst.

But to her surprise, Peter chuckled right along with him. "Yes, that was probably not the best first impression I've ever made, but it was probably the most memorable."

An uncomfortable smirk crossed her father's face, and Alex had to hide her delight. She unbuttoned her coat and smiled at Peter as he helped her remove it, his hands grazing her shoulders. Then he handed it to the uniformed woman who, as all good help should be according to her mother, was lurking just outside the room, ready to pounce whenever she was needed.

"Thank you," Peter replied as he took off his own coat and handed it to her as well. The woman smiled politely, and she was gone.

Alex didn't recognize her, though she knew for a fact that she was not the same woman who had been here over the holidays. It wasn't a surprise. Susan Sanders fired the help almost as soon as she hired them. She didn't like anyone getting too comfortable at her house, not even company.

Her mother walked past where they stood and into

the living room, pausing at its doorway, "We are so happy you could make it. Howard, where are the few manners you have, offer Dr. Gibson a drink."

Howard Sanders rolled his eyes at his wife, but seeing that his glass was now empty, he dutifully walked into the living room to the bar. Then after refilling his own, he dutifully asked, "What can I get you? Alex, a martini, I assume?"

"The stronger the better," she muttered under her breath as she nodded to her father.

"Scotch, on the rocks, sir," Peter replied as he walked across the room to get the drinks, leaving Alex alone with her mother.

She looked down at the green dress she had chosen for tonight, which was actually appropriate for this occasion. Usually, she felt quite attractive in it, but for some reason, tonight she felt like she was wearing a gunnysack.

"You look rather nice this evening, darling," her mother purred, to her amazement. It made her nervous to have her mother compliment her. It was out of character, but then, "Dr. Gibson must be a good influence on you, but apparently not entirely. Those shoes are simply awful."

Alex shot her mother a look and was about to snap back at her when Peter appeared beside her and handed her a crystal martini glass with a sterling toothpick as long as her finger full of olives. She took a sip, happy to know she had a weapon if she needed it.

"The shoes were my suggestion," Peter said easily as he slipped his arm around her waist. "Her ankle isn't quite ready for heels just yet. But isn't she exquisite in green?"

Nicely done, Alex thought. He'd put her mother in

her place and he had reminded her that he was a doctor all in one sentence. Alex relaxed back into him and smiled sweetly at her mother. "Peter is always looking out for me," she volleyed back, which was true.

Susan Sanders looked at them inquisitively, as though she was trying to use some unsaid power to get to the truth.

"Yes, I must say, Alex, the change in you is remarkable. The fact that you have gone from being adamantly against any type of relationship to head over heels for someone. Not to mention someone so, shall I say, *acceptable.* Your father and I couldn't be more surprised or pleased."

There it was, though no one other than Alex would have gotten the subtle challenge. Pleasing her parents was something that Alex had avoided for some time. This was her mother's way of calling her out, and it took all her strength not to spill the truth just to tick her off.

Then something clicked in Alex, and she suddenly realized she could pull this off. Because it would blow her mother away when she realized she'd been tricked. The rules of their relationship had been long established, and she was about to turn them on their ear. Her mother wasn't going to know which way was up.

"You know what they say about finding the right person. It can change your point of view about everything," she said, smiling at Peter adoringly.

"I hope this means we'll see you more often at all the important events. Not having a date is no longer an excuse, I dare say." Her mother's hand went to her pearls as she spoke, and her head tilted in her standard pose. "As a matter of fact, there is a benefit for the ballet just around the corner. It would be the perfect opportunity to introduce your new suitor to your friends."

"They're your friends, mother, not mine," Alex quipped before she could stop herself.

"Are you talking about the Black and White Ball?" Peter inquired easily.

Alex turned her head sharply to look at him, surprised he would know such a thing. He must have really done some research for this dinner.

"Yes, that's exactly what I was speaking of, Dr. Gibson." Her voice oozed with pleasure.

"Mrs. Sanders, please, call me Peter." He smiled at her.

"I'll do my best," she tittered, laying her hand on Peter's arm. "But 'doctor' sounds so nice."

Alex turned so that her mother wouldn't see her roll her eyes, and walked across the room toward where her father still stood behind the bar. Obviously, her mother didn't need to be won over. She was too busy fawning over Peter and asking him about every social event on her calendar. Peter seemed to be holding his own, though. Which was surprising in and of itself. Nobody knew Chicago society like Susan Sanders—which events were necessary to attend and which you shouldn't be caught dead at. It seemed odd that Peter should know all the right answers, based on what Alex knew about him.

"Shall we join them?" her father asked, sidling up next to her.

Her mind swimming with all the things that might go wrong, she could only nod.

"That's what drew me to Alex the first time I met

her—her independence and individuality," Peter was saying as Alex approached them. "She's no cookie-cutter society girl. She can stand on her own." His sincerity took her by surprise, and she had to admit she liked it, but one look at her mother and it was obvious the feeling was not mutual.

"Yes, well, Alex has always been her own girl." Her voice broke as she said it, and her hand went to her pearls in an attempt to ease her throat. Luckily, they were all saved from whatever awkward thing might have been said next. The new hired help appeared.

"Dinner is served," she said, her voice rich with boredom.

Her days here are numbered, Alex thought to herself.

Her mother brushed by them, eager to make sure everything was in place, leaving Alex and Peter alone for a brief moment.

"You must have really studied up on the whole society thing. You're really talking her language. Nice work," Alex whispered as they walked toward the dining room.

"Just trying to be the perfect catch." He smiled, and his eyes sparkled mischievously. "Not much she can object to."

"Except for that whole independent woman thing—that made her head spin." Alex suppressed a giggle.

"Well, I'm an honest man, and I had to throw a dose of the truth at her, to ease my conscience about this whole charade."

Alex wanted to ask what he was telling the truth about—her independent spirit or his attraction to her—but they were already at the table. Peter pulled her chair out for her and she sat. Then he did the same for her mother, who practically beamed as she sat, before taking a crack at her husband.

"It is so nice to have a man in the house who knows the social graces a woman appreciates." She pursed her lips as she looked down the table at Howard Sanders.

"Well, you know what they say about turning a sow's ear into a silk purse, Susan," he quipped, a sneer on his face.

"Alex, I am just so impressed with this change that has come over you," her mother said, ignoring her husband's sarcastic remark. "I couldn't be more pleased."

She took her perfectly folded napkin off the table and placed it in her lap. Alex had to admit that she was pretty impressed, too. Peter was handling things perfectly, and Susan Sanders's dinner parties were a difficult field to navigate.

Their food arrived in perfectly timed courses, one more delicious than the next, and the evening progressed in a smooth manner that Alex was not accustomed to in her parents' home. Though the conversation was light and somewhat meaningless, it did move along without any more hostility. Even her parents seemed to have called an uneasy truce. That in itself was something seldom seen. If she had been in therapy, this evening would have cost her a few hundred dollars to sort out.

They were just finishing dessert and coffee when Peter's cell phone rang. It was a planned call from Claire so they could make an early exit. He excused himself to take the call, and Alex had to sit on her hands to keep from getting up to get her coat, knowing the end was near. All this polite banter was freaking her out.

"Well, Alex, I have taken under consideration that you are finally making appropriate choices in your life. I see no reason that you have to close your little shop. Just don't let it take too much of your time away from your darling Peter." Her mother smiled as though she had just awarded Alex the Nobel Peace Prize.

There was that word "little" again, attached to her life's work, no less. However, Alex was able to maintain her composure. She had won round one.

Peter swept into the room. "I'm sorry, but I've been called in to the hospital. We'll need to be going. I do apologize. Mr. Sanders. I'll take a rain check on that brandy, and we never did get to discuss the Cubs' outlook for this year. Alex tells me you are a big fan." He helped Alex from her chair, and the maid appeared with their coats before her parents had a chance to even stand.

"Thank you for this superb dinner and for raising such an amazing daughter. Alex is really special." He pulled her back against him and wrapped his arms around her waist, and she felt her knees go a little weak as she smiled sweetly at her mother.

Her mother's face glowed as was expected, but as Alex looked at her father, she was surprised to see a look of admiration on his face, too. It seemed that Peter had the entire Sanders family under his spell. As they said their good-nights and stepped out into the frosty night, Alex was feeling things she had never felt before. For the first time in her life, she wasn't terrified by them.

Chapter Eighteen

"So, tell me *again* what Peter said to your mother about his attraction to you." Claire was rambling on and on, making Alex wish for the millionth time she had kept her mouth shut about the dinner with her parents.

They were fighting the crowds of brides-to-be and the February chill on their way into the Chicago Bridal Fair. That in and of itself was enough to put Alex on edge—all those happy women looking to hammer out the details of one glorious day, without bothering to consider what it meant for the rest of their lives. Alex had to push her feelings about the state of marriage out of her head just to walk through the door.

Claire was unrelenting on dissecting every last detail of the dinner and the feelings it stirred up. Alex was just as eager to ignore the whole thing, especially the feelings part. The giddiness that filled her every time she thought about Peter was perturbing. At this point, she didn't need the distraction. Especially now that she and Claire were about to go into covert action—infiltrating this bridal fair and drumming up some business without getting caught. She had to focus.

Just as they reached the front of the line and purchased their tickets, Alex shot Claire a look that finally seemed to get her point across. They were through discussing the dinner.

"We need to case the joint, find someplace out of the way so we can show off our samples without causing a scene," Claire whispered as they checked their coats.

"Case the joint?" Alex asked, suppressing a giggle. Claire certainly was getting into the spirit of this little adventure.

"You know, look around, and see where the best place to set up shop . . ."

Alex gasped. "Do you think we should use aliases?"

"Don't be ridiculous. The point of being here is getting your name out. If you use a fake one, it defeats our entire purpose!"

Alex looked at her in disbelief. Obviously, her attempt at humor had been lost on Claire. She was just about to point out that she was kidding, but Claire had already turned to begin wading her way through the crowd in search of the perfect location. Alex shook her head and dove in behind her, trying to follow.

As they weaved in and out of groups of women, some of them still girls, really, they passed displays highlighting every detail of a wedding. The wide-eyed masses were flocking to them. No detail was too small to be overlooked. There were golf ball favors, musical garter belts, even matching bride and groom underwear. Alex couldn't believe what she was seeing.

The delicious smells seeping out from the booths made it clear they had made their way into the catering section of the bridal extravaganza. Silver trays adorned the arms of men and women who roamed, trying to entice the crowd to step closer and take a sample.

Claire and Alex rounded the corner at the end of the row, and suddenly tables, full of cakes so beautiful and intricate it was hard to believe they were actually edible, surrounded them. Alex longed to stick her finger in the side of one and sample the frosting, but was afraid of what her partner might do if she stopped.

Just past the cakes, Alex lost track of Claire. Distracted by a sudden blast of music from a DJ beckoning the blushing masses to a small dance floor to do some boogying, Alex froze in her tracks. It only took that split second for Claire to disappear. Throngs of women rushed past Alex, apparently not wanting to miss the opportunity to show each other their moves.

"This may actually be worse than I imagined," Alex muttered as she stood on her tiptoes trying to catch a glimpse of Claire. It was impossible to believe that people had actually dreamed up some of the gimmicks she was seeing around her.

The invitation booths offered things that were predictable. White, square, engraved cards printed with black ink. She paused; maybe that was what everyone wanted—traditional, boring invitations. Panic rose in her throat. Maybe this wasn't the answer. It could be that no one here *wanted* anything original.

Just as she was about to throw in the towel, Claire appeared out of nowhere, red-faced and panting as though she'd run a mile. She grabbed Alex by the elbow, spun her around and pushed her through the crowd until they popped out at the other side of the room. After darting behind an elaborate floral display, they stopped in front of what appeared to be a janitor's closet.

"Well it took some real leg work, but I finally found us this spot. It's perfect, don't you think?" Claire said, satisfaction in her voice, her eyes wide, and her smile even wider.

Alex looked around her. She wasn't sure exactly which spot Claire was talking about. "You mean this area here behind the florists? It's not very big, and you know me—there is the chance I could fall through that drapery at the back and cause quite a scene."

Claire didn't speak; she just rolled her eyes and motioned for Alex to follow her as she turned the knob on the closet door and, in her best Vanna White imitation, motioned to the dusty space in grand fashion.

"A closet?" Alex could feel her face scrunching up in bewilderment. "This is the perfect spot you were thinking of when you concocted this plan? Don't you think these girls are going to notice that we're in a closet? They don't seem like the brightest bunch, but I do think they'll be able to tell the difference between one of those fancy booths and a closet!"

Claire crossed her arms over her chest, and Alex knew that any arguing was futile at this point. Her mind was made up, that was all there was to it.

Claire waved her hands to shush Alex. "We can't exactly do this out in the open. The organizers of this thing will throw us out on our respective behinds if they catch us doing business without one of those fancy ID cards everyone is wearing."

Alex stood as firm as possible. "But Claire, this is a closet!"

Hands on her hips, Claire replied, "It's got to be secluded and well lit, and *this* fit the bill. Plus, I thought the floral booths did a nice job of masking the mildew smell from where the fire-hose leaked."

Alex blinked at Claire's warped sense of reality. She spoke so matter-of-factly, it almost seemed logical.

"Don't dwell," Claire snapped. "Pull yourself together and get ready. I'm going to commandeer us some clients!" With that, she was gone, swallowed up by a colorful display of roses and lilies—leaving Alex with nothing to do but lean against the door of her new "booth" and wait.

She didn't have long to wait, as it turned out: Claire returned with a fresh-faced young woman in tow just minutes later.

"Now," Claire was saying, keeping a firm hand on the back of the young blond. "If you want to set a mood for your big day, you don't want what everyone else is having, now do you?" The petite little thing nodded in agreement.

They came to a stop in front of where Alex stood, her arms crossed across her chest.

"This is Alex Sanders." Claire beamed with pride. "And if you can imagine it, she can create it. You're on your way to getting something really unique." She said the last bit like some sort of proclamation and once again disappeared behind the flower display, raining petals in her wake.

Alex stared at the girl, who was looking a bit like a lamb led to slaughter. It took a minute before she snapped into Correspondence mode and ushered her into the closet to look at her portfolio.

"Um, as my associate told you, we specialize in unique invitations, and also offer the whole package of the things you need—shower invitations, programs, and thank-you notes." Alex stammered through her rehearsed speech as she fumbled to open her sample book. Her head banged into the light bulb that hung from the ceiling as she spoke.

The girl looked at her, bewildered. "Are we in a closet?" she asked in a small voice.

"Yes, well," Alex coughed. "A unique line of invitations deserves a unique presentation, doesn't it?"

What a load of garbage! Alex thought as she rambled on. Nevertheless, the girl seemed to be falling for it, so she continued.

"We didn't want to be out there among all those cookie-cutter booths. Correspondence doesn't need all that to highlight our samples. They speak for themselves." With that, she finally managed to get her sample book open without spilling its contents, and she handed it to the young woman.

Strains of "the hustle" filtered in through the door. Wedding-land raced along outside their little closet, and for a moment, Alex wondered if Claire had bothered to check to see if the door had an automatic lock. What if she and this prospective customer were trapped until Claire returned with her next victim?

As slyly as she could, Alex shifted to the other side of the woman and felt for the knob behind her.

Thankfully, it turned when she twisted it. She let out a sigh of relief as the woman let out a squeal that took Alex completely by surprise. She jumped and banged her head into the light bulb again.

She just hadn't expected a noise like that to come out

of such a pristine-looking thing. Well, they did always say it was the quiet ones you had to worry about.

Alex looked over her shoulder to see what, exactly, had caused the woman to erupt. She was looking at the sample printed on pressed-leaf paper. Well then, at least the sound was justified. That invitation was something to behold, and, Alex noted, quite costly.

Maybe this was going to work after all.

"This is exactly what I want. It's perfect. My fiancé just loves trees!"

Of course he does, Alex thought to herself but responded with an enthusiastic, "Who doesn't?"

"So, how do I order them?" she bubbled on. Do you have a form or something I can fill out?"

"Well, let's invite your fiancé to my shop for a meeting so we can choose exactly what you both want. If you wouldn't mind just jotting down your name and a number where I can reach you . . ." Alex handed her a pen and clipboard. Once the bride-to-be handed it back, Alex gave her one of her business cards. Before Alex knew what hit her, the woman had pulled her into a hug.

"You just don't know how much these invitations mean to me. Robert is going to just love them. You are amazing! All of these, well, they're just beautiful. I don't know how to thank you." She pulled Alex back into another hug.

"You're welcome," Alex said, forcing the tiny thing to arms' distance. She felt an odd sort of satisfaction with all this praise. However, to be proud of this work made her uncomfortable. Unsure what to say, she just returned the girl's sweet smile and stared at her blankly. Finally, the door opened, and there stood Claire with their next blushing bride.

It went on that way for hours. Alex had never been hugged so much in her life, and if she heard the word fiancé one more time, she thought her head might possibly explode. But the overwhelming positive response they were getting was beyond what they had imagined. Claire was right—some of these people were actually looking for something original. By the fifth pretty young thing, Alex had even managed to perfect her smile and quiet the nagging voices in her head.

Three hours later, things started to slow down a little. Alex was relieved to step out of the closet and catch a breath of fresh air. The big fashion show was about to start, and the women were elbowing one another to try to get a good view of the runway.

"So we'll wait around for the fashion show to be over and see if we can grab a few more customers. Then we can scoot out of here," Claire said, handing Alex one of the glasses of champagne she had snagged from a passing waiter.

"Did you want to try and check it out?" She nodded her head in the direction of the stage.

Alex shot her a scathing look that served as her definitive answer.

Claire shrugged and raised her glass. "Cheers!"

They clinked glasses, both of them sighing at their moment's peace. Alex closed her tired eyes, tuning out Claire's enthusiasm and the continuous strain of the wedding march booming over the PA system. She raised the glass to her lips, the bubbles tickling her nose, and felt at peace.

Claire's sharp elbow snapped her out of it. She opened her eyes and saw, over the rim of the plastic glass, what she knew was trouble heading right toward them. A woman with one of those ID cards around her neck was talking to a security guard and pointing in their general direction.

Chapter Nineteen

"**I** think our little gig is up," Alex said to Claire out of the corner of her mouth, nodding as inconspicuously as she could toward the guard.

Claire stood wide-eyed and silent, but as soon as she laid eyes on the rent-a-cop headed their way, she was on her toes, ready to retreat. Together they turned and tried to make a break for it, but they ran directly into the thick mass of women lining up for the fashion show. Since there was no chance for escape, they turned to face the long arm of the Bridal Fair Law.

"Ladies," he began his deep voice a perfect match for the mountain of a man that he was. "I've been getting complaints of some unlicensed vendors working at this end of the floor. You wouldn't know anything about that, would you?"

"Us? No! We were just trying to see the fashion show," Claire squeaked.

Way to keep your cool, Claire, Alex thought to herself.

The officer wasn't buying it. He hooked his thumbs

around the black belt partially hidden by his enormous belly. His cold dark eyes settled on Alex. "What do you have there?" he asked, pointing toward the portfolio under her arm.

"Wedding plans?" she said as innocently as she could, but as luck would have it, there was a surge in the crowd behind her and she was pushed forward, losing her grip on the folder. It hit the floor, invitations spilling out at the security guard's feet.

Claire scrambled to pick them up, but it was too late—their cover was blown.

"I'm going to have to escort you from the premises," he said matter-of-factly, obviously thrilled to have some sort of official duty to perform.

He maneuvered them through the crowd, a firm grip on both of their arms. Alex felt her face flush with embarrassment.

"We need to get our coats." Alex wrenched her arm free from his grasp. She expected him to protest, but he just shrugged his shoulders and crossed his arms in front of his chest, his arms resting to some extent on his stomach.

Claire fished the claim tickets out of her purse and went to retrieve their coats as the guard stood watch. Alex rubbed at the sore spot left on her arm. She couldn't be annoyed—he was just doing his job, after all.

"Kind of a rowdy crowd, huh?" She tried to joke, but his face remained unchanged by her attempt at humor. Embarrassed for the second time in as many minutes, she dropped her eyes from his surly face. They came to rest on a shirt button that was doing its best to hold the blue polyester fabric together.

Thankfully, Claire returned with their coats in a

flash. After pulling hers on, Alex tried again to apolo-gize again for breaking the rules, but to no avail—this guy didn't care one way or the other about her apology. He had a job to do.

They had just about reached the door when a voice, so like her mother's, stopped Alex dead in her tracks.

"Excuse me, sir! You'll need to wait one second." The tone dripped of a good upbringing, and Alex was sure that when she turned around, she would see the coordinator of the event ready to lay into her for this breach of etiquette.

Instead, she stood face to face with a young woman whom Alex's mother would have died to have for a daughter. Straight blond hair, cut in a sleek bob, held in place by a plaid hair band that complemented the designer navy suit she was wearing.

She looked directly at Alex and said, "I heard you were presenting some unique invitations. I simply must see them."

Alex knew immediately that this was a girl who always got her way, and her hackles went up. Before she could reply, the guard interrupted.

"Ma'am, I am sorry, but these young ladies are leav-ing. Any business you have with them—"

The young woman waved him off. "Nonsense. I am planning *the* wedding of the season, and I need invita-tions that will make a statement. If this woman can pro-vide them, I *am* going to see them," she insisted. With that, the rent-a-cop shrugged like it was no skin off his nose and retreated.

Alex's mouth popped open in amazement. Maybe she should have paid more attention in those society classes her mother made her take on Saturdays. This girl did know how to get what she wanted. Alex looked around and spied a bench near the entrance.

"Well, let's take a seat," she said, pointing toward the bench. The young woman turned on her heel and led the way. Alex flashed Claire a look of bewilderment, but she just shrugged her shoulders. Apparently, she didn't know what to make of this perfect young thing, either.

Ms. Debutante sat down, perched really, on the edge of the bench, her posture straight as an arrow, her ankles crossed neatly behind one another, her matching navy blue shoes shining in the way that only expensive shoes can.

Nervously, Alex sat down and pulled out her portfolio. "Here, let me," the woman said as she grabbed it out of her hands before Alex could utter a word.

It took Alex a minute to comprehend what had just happened. She had seen her mother do it to servants repeatedly, but no one had ever treated Alex in such a way.

All the awe she felt flew right out the window as Alex was struck with a sense of déjà vu. This woman was a carbon copy of the snotty girls her mother had forced her to spend time with at the club's young women affairs. If there was one lesson Alex had learned at those events, it was that all that snootiness didn't come cheap. This girl had money, and money was what Alex needed.

Summoning all the strength she had left after this crazy day, Alex swallowed hard, and the voice she managed came out surprisingly pleasant.

"So as you can see, we do some really unique things, and we offer a wide variety of options. We can meet

whatever your needs may be: shower invitations, programs, place cards—you name it."

The woman didn't speak, but rather sat very seriously, flipping the pages of the portfolio in her lap. Her
face expressed no emotion as she studied them one by
one, painfully slowly.

When she had finally finished inspecting the book,
she snapped it closed and held it out for Alex to take,
flashing her perfectly manicured fingernails—French,
of course.

"Yes, I see some things in there that would more than
suit my needs." She smiled in that oh-so-polite way that
women of her social stature do. A sort of "I know you
are below me but I am currently in need of your ser-
vices" way.

"I will need over five hundred, and that number is
for the wedding invitations alone. Will you be able to
meet that order?" Her gaze took them both in, sizing
them up.

She said it so calmly, so brazenly. It struck Alex how
opposite she was from the other brides Alex had seen
that day. Nope, this girl was definitely not a hugger.

The large number repeated itself over and over in her
stunned mind, but she didn't want to show her shock.
"That shouldn't be a problem for us. As I said, we offer
an entire line of coordinating invitations for your showers or engagement parties. Not to mention all the things
you'll need for the ceremony and reception."

She finished her little speech in one breath. Then she
reached into the pocket of her portfolio for one of her
business cards, but before she could even hand it to the
woman, one was being pushed into her hand.

"Call me at this number, and we will set up a meeting

to discuss the details," she said matter-of-factly as she stood. Her hands brushed at her skirt to straighten out the nonexistent wrinkles. Their meeting was apparently over.

Not to be outdone, Alex forced her own card into the woman's hand. A tight smile plastered on her face.

"Your fiancé will be joining you, then?" Alex asked, her blood curdling from all the society trappings exuding from her new client.

"Oh no. He's very busy, and very important. He's going to be chief of Emergency Medicine at Mercy Hospital someday. He can't be bothered with these kinds of details." She tossed her head back and laughed at the ridiculousness of Alex's statement, a polite society laugh that expressed no real delight or amusement.

Of course he is. Alex bit her tongue for what seemed like the hundredth time since they'd met. This time, before she could make a sarcastic remark, the woman saved herself. She dropped the final detail that let Alex know she had pegged this society girl correctly.

"My mother will be joining me," she said matter-of-factly.

Alex nodded knowingly. Of course, the society wedding of the season would have a society mother to go along with it. She glanced again at the girl's perfectly manicured hand and noticed it was missing an important detail—an engagement ring.

"Well, if he can't be there, will you be able to bring your ring so I can get some idea of his taste?" she asked innocently.

Color rushed to the girl's cheeks. "As I said earlier, he can't be bothered with the details. We're still looking for the perfect ring, but trust me, I know his taste."

Then she was gone, leaving Claire and Alex staring after her.

"She was an interesting one."

That Claire, always trying to say something positive. Alex rolled her eyes. " 'Interesting' isn't the first word that comes to my mind."

"Well, if she comes up with the kind of numbers she's throwing around, we could have the money you need for that down payment from her order alone," Claire said as they bundled up to face the cold.

That was true. As annoying as she was, her society wedding of the season would be the answer to Alex's prayers.

"If I don't kill her first," she muttered as she looked at the crisp, cream card in her hand:

Ashleigh Rogers
312-778-2126

What kind of person carries a personal card? she thought as she shoved it into her pocket. But she knew the answer—*her worst nightmare in designer clothes, that's who.*

She pulled her warm woolen mittens on and gave Claire a smile. As the cold air hit them in the face, a sense of hope Alex hadn't had in weeks filled her chest. She might just be able to save her shop, after all.

Chapter Twenty

"I called Stephen and he's going to meet us here," Claire said, taking the pitcher of beer out of Alex's hand and setting it on the table in front of her.

Alex clanked the mugs she was holding in her other hand down next to the pitcher and slid into the booth across from Claire. "Good—he should be able to help us figure out how much revenue we generated today." They were at Izzy's, having an impromptu celebration of sorts.

Claire picked up the pitcher and filled their glasses. Handing one to Alex, she raised her own in the air. "Mission accomplished! Here's to us!"

They clinked their glasses together, both smiling broadly.

"You do realize that we haven't really sold anything, right? That the real work is still ahead of us?" Alex asked, setting her mug down on the worn table in front of her after she'd takes a sip.

"Don't be a spoil sport." Claire furrowed her brow.

"Of course I know we have a lot of work ahead of us, but can't we just enjoy this little victory?"

"Actually, yes, I think we can." Alex took another drink of her beer and leaned back in her seat.

"So, what did you think of our little socialite?" Claire asked, her eyes sparkling.

Alex waved her hand in front of her. "I think we should take a break from shop talk for a while. Stephen is going to want to hear all about it when he gets here, anyway." She paused, noting the twinkle that had appeared in Claire's eyes.

"And speaking of Stephen, I think I've done a pretty good job minding my own business, but enough is enough—spill it, girl!"

Claire's mouth dropped open in mock shock and then broke into a wide grin. "I don't know where to start, Alex. It's—it's . . ." She paused, searching for the right word. "Just wonderful!" she exclaimed. "He's just wonderful."

"Wonderful," Alex repeated, taking a drink of her beer.

"Well, he's Stephen, so you know what a great guy he is."

"Claire, of course I know what a great guy he is, and obviously you two are wonderful together. One look at you tells me that."

She looked past Claire at the group of people talking in the booth behind them, two men and two women. Two couples. Why was it that suddenly everywhere she looked, she saw couples? More important, why didn't she find it as annoying as she used to?

"What I want to know is how did you go from being the girl he gets coffee for every Tuesday to the girl that makes his dreams come true?"

Alex didn't know why it was suddenly so important for her to understand. Maybe it was spending an entire day at the mothership of commitment. More than anything in the world, she wanted to understand why and how Claire and Stephen had gotten together. Obviously, it agreed with both of them. Aside from Claire's little foray into dictatorship today, she had been practically giddy for weeks.

Claire tilted her head. "Oh, Alex, that's the thing about it. I can't tell you how it happened, just that it did. The more time we spent together, the better friends we became, and then one day, bam!" She clapped her hands together. "Both of us knew that we were more than just friends. Stephen and I are happy because we are ourselves, and we actually like each other."

"I couldn't have said it better." Stephen had appeared beside them. He leaned over and kissed Claire on the cheek, and the two of them stared at each other, smiling.

Alex was surprised to find that she didn't automatically feel the need to poke fun at them. It was probably because they were still just Claire and Stephen, her two closest friends. They hadn't suddenly morphed into some lovesick, ooey-gooey couple who didn't resemble themselves.

"Well, if this celebration is to continue, we'll need more to drink." He walked the short distance to the bar and motioned for the bartender to fill the pitcher.

"It's finding the person that likes you for who you are and doesn't want you to become their version of you. That's the only trick," Claire said, her eyes never leaving Stephen.

Alex nodded, though she knew Claire didn't see her.

That might actually be the easy part. If there was one thing Alex knew, it was who she was.

Peter has seen the real me, the clumsy, irrational me, Alex thought. *And he didn't seem to mind; he actually seemed to like who I am.* Maybe there was more there than she was willing to admit.

Stephen set the now full pitcher on the table and slid into the booth next to Claire.

"So tell me all about it. Was your mission a success?" he said, sincere interest in his voice.

She leaned back and listened as Claire gave a replay of their day in bridal land. She didn't skip a detail, and Stephen hung on every word, laughing as she described the coat closet and the security guard. Through the whole thing, Alex sat silently observing her friends, feeling the change that was coming over her.

Sitting across the table of this bar, where they had sat so many times together before, was the couple who might actually prove her theory about relationships wrong. Though it filled her with a sense of nervous energy, there was no sign of panic. That was a change. She allowed herself for just a moment to linger on the idea that Peter might have something to do with it, too. Though she didn't for the life of her know why she was coming to this conclusion today.

She downed the rest of her beer in one gulp and set it down on the table. "Refill, please!"

"So, the celebration is on then, I take it?" Stephen lifted the pitcher and poured her the perfect glass of beer with just the right amount of foam.

"Well, we do have a lot to celebrate. First, there's the infiltration of the bridal fair. Then there are you two, all blissfully happy and *normal*."

"I'm not sure why you'd be celebrating the fact that we're normal," Stephen countered with a smirk on his face.

"Well, I guess it's more the fact that it doesn't freak me out. So anyway, yes, the celebration is on! Cheers!"

"Cheers!" Her friends joined in—Claire enthusiastically, Stephen a bit perplexed, but smiling nonetheless.

From that point on, the beer flowed freely and the three of them laughed and talked. For the first time in a long time, Alex didn't feel as though the weight of the world was on her shoulders. Late in the evening, she excused herself to the restroom. Standing for the first time, she realized just how much beer she had consumed.

"Are you all right?" Claire asked as she swayed.

"I'm not driving, just going to the girls' room." Alex giggled in one of those "when-I'm-drunk-I'm-hilarious" moments.

Apparently she really was comical, because Claire erupted into giggles herself.

Alex wound her way through the crowds of people that lined the bar. She walked past the pool table and dartboards, until finally she reached the little hallway that led to the bathrooms.

It was dark and a little dingy, but she could definitely make out the shape of a couple in the corner. In her hazy mind, she had to tell herself not to pause and stare, as intrigued as she suddenly was by couples. Luckily, there was no line for the bathroom, so she was in and out fast, her presence not disturbing the groping going on in the hallway outside.

Just as she reached the bar, she thought she saw a familiar face at the entrance.

Alex screwed up her eyes to try to get him into focus.

Julie Stone

His sudden movement in her direction had caused everything to go blurry.

"Peter!"

She raced to where Peter stood, just inside the door, looking around the crowded bar.

"Peter, what are you doing here?" Alex said, throwing herself into his arms.

"Stephen called me, said you were celebrating." Peter smiled at her and wrapped his arms around her waist. She took it as an embrace, but quickly realized it was really more of an attempt to steady her.

"I can see you have been taking the celebrating seriously." He laughed.

In that moment, the smile on his lips, warmth spread through her as he held her in his arms. Alex knew Peter *was* the reason she was contemplating relationships. She also knew if she took even a second to think about it, her courage would falter. So she took a deep breath, and kissed him. Not the desperate-for-physical-contact kiss she had planted on him that first night, but a soft, intimate one, that spoke of things to come.

Peter looked down at her, happy surprise in his eyes. That was a step in the right direction. At least he hadn't turned to run.

"Peter, I need to tell you something," she started, but he put his fingers to her lips and then kissed her again. Her knees seemed to go out from under her, and she was glad he had his arms around her waist or this perfect moment would be ruined by yet another fall.

He pulled back and looked deep into her eyes. "I think you've had enough of this celebration. How about I take you home?" he whispered in her ear, his warm breath sending shivers down her spine.

Alex nodded, scared that if she opened her mouth, she would ruin this. The last thing she wanted was to send Peter on his way. No, for once in her life, Alex Sanders was going to use her heart, not her head.

Chapter Twenty-one

"Home sweet home," Peter announced as he pushed his way through Alex's front door. Alex, whom he held in his arms, giggled at something. He wasn't sure what was so funny, but whatever it was had caused her to collapse outside the building on the sidewalk. After a few minutes of trying to reason with her, he'd eventually just picked her up and carried her in.

He crossed the room and deposited her on the couch, reaching across to flick on the lamp on the table. He hadn't realized how close they were until the dim light from the lamp cast his shadow across her face. Alex pulled her hair out of her face and looked him in the eye, their faces inches apart.

Peter inhaled deeply. *She is so beautiful,* he thought.

"Peter, there's something I need to tell you," she said, the slur of her words reminding him that she was in no condition to follow through on that kiss at the bar. He stood up to put some distance between them.

"I don't know if this is a great time for you to tell me

anything. You may regret it in the morning." He smiled at the look of confusion that crossed her face.

"Peter, sit down here." She patted the couch next to where she sat. Her coat, scarf, and mittens were still on, the moss green color of them catching the flecks in her eyes. "I *need* to tell you something."

She looked up at him, and he wanted to comply. But to sit next to her when the taste of her was still on his lips, the memory of her in his arms still strong—it was too tempting. He'd already taken it farther then he should, kissing her in the bar.

"Alex, let's get your coat off and make some coffee. When you sober up, then we'll talk." Reasoning with her was a gamble, he realized. He'd tried it once before, out on the sidewalk, and that hadn't gotten him anywhere.

"I'm sober enough to *talk,* Peter!" she said emphatically as she stood to take off her coat, but then the zipper got caught in her scarf. She tugged at it emphatically, but that threw her notorious balance off-kilter. She slumped back onto the couch, took off her mittens, and began unwrapping the scarf from her neck. But it was still caught in the zipper.

He chuckled to himself, as any sober observer would, and then against his better judgment, he moved nearer to her. *Just to help her with the scarf,* he reasoned.

Leaning across her, he moved her small, cold hands away, and with the skill of, well, a doctor, removed the offending scarf and tugged the zipper down. Their eyes locked in a gaze that sent shivers down his arms. Alex stood to shrug off the coat, swaying a bit before she caught herself by grabbing onto Peter's shoulders.

"My hero," she said softly, with just a hint of slur.

"That's what I wanted to tell you. You're my hero, like in an old movie. You came out of nowhere and helped me save my store, and now," she paused and tipped her head back to meet his gaze, her eyes a little glazed.

"Now, somehow you've managed to change my mind about relationships, men, and the general insincerity of love. And you know what? I'm not the least bit scared about it."

"The general insincerity of love." He smiled because she had done the same for him, and he hadn't even known he had a problem with love.

"Yep." Her hands trailed up his shoulders, clasping behind his neck. "I think we should celebrate, don't you?" She put her hands on the back of his head and pulled his mouth toward hers.

It's just a kiss, he tried to reason, as his mouth found hers, eager to feel her soft lips again. But as she melted into him, her entire body pressed to his. He knew it was much more that that.

"Alex." He said her name in a way that he hoped would not be confused with a cry of passion, but rather would be heard as an attention-getter.

"Alex," he said again, with a little more force and a little less lust.

"We need to stop," he said, summoning all the willpower he had.

"I'm not that drunk," she said, and then giggled.

"Of course not," he said, holding her hands firmly in his. "That's not what I meant. It's just that, you've rid yourself of what was keeping us apart. Now I need to do the same." He couldn't help it; he kissed the smooth skin of her hand, and looked her deep in the eyes. "Then we can be together, really together."

He hoped beyond hope that she wouldn't ask him what was keeping him from her. Telling her about Ashleigh was something he knew he had to do, but not tonight. His little bit of honesty would have to be enough.

Alex sighed. "Fine," she relented. "But get rid of whatever it is quickly, before all this freaks me out."

She flopped back on the couch, the temptress she had been gone in a flash as she curled up and pulled the blanket from the back. "I'm a little sleepy, anyway."

With another small sigh, she was asleep. Peter stared at her in amazement. He had a feeling that he had been looking for Alex Sanders his whole life without knowing it.

He pulled the blanket up around her shoulders and then zipped up his own coat.

There was a tap on the door.

Opening it, he was not surprised to find Claire on the other side. He didn't know her all that well, but no woman would let her drunk friend go home with a guy and not at least check on her later.

"Alex forgot this." She held up a black purse and craned her neck around, trying to see past him. "Where is she?"

He stepped aside to let her in. "I'm sure that would have put her in a panic in the morning." He took the purse from Claire and set it on the hall table, then pointed toward the living room.

"You're leaving?" Claire glanced at the couch, where soft snores were now escaping Alex.

"You have great timing, actually. I wasn't sure how I was going to get the door to lock when I left."

"Alex sure was having a good time tonight. The bridal fair was today, and I think we may have met the answer to our prayers—some society girl, having the wedding of the season. Alex was thrilled," Claire explained.

Peter nodded, finding it hard to get a word in.

Claire continued, "Listen, I realize this isn't my place, but Alex is really great. And, well, whether she'll admit it or not, she thinks you are, too. So be patient with her."

"Claire, I can assure you, patience is one of my best qualities, especially when it comes to Alex. Do you mind staying with her?"

"Not at all." Claire smiled. "That way I can get her side of the story as soon as she wakes up! That is, if she remembers any of it."

Peter shook his head as he showed himself to the door. "Good night, Claire," he said with a laugh.

He stepped out to the dimly lit street, his mind racing with all of the possibilities the evening could have held. It was just as well; he still had his involvement with Ashleigh to resolve. *Involvement*—that's what he was calling it now, downgrading it from a relationship.

He walked toward the train, feeling the urgency of his situation. His plan was in motion; he was working more hours and making himself unavailable to Ashleigh. He had even managed to introduce her to Michael once when she stopped by the hospital.

Michael had really turned on the charm, as he always did when he talked to anyone with prestige or power. Ashleigh had bought right into it, eating up his compliments.

Peter had hope that in the end, they would all get what they wanted without anyone getting hurt. Actually, he was hoping for more than that. Michael and Ashleigh were a perfect fit, once he removed himself from the equation. He just knew they would fall for each other.

When that happened, he and Alex could finish where that kiss had left off. That thought was enough to warm him as he walked through the dark February night.

Chapter Twenty-two

There was a monkey perched on Alex's shoulders, pounding on her head as if it was a pair of bongo drums. She was spinning around, trying to grab it without much luck, the result being that she was dizzy and somewhat nauseated. In the distance, a low rumble and blasting of a train whistle stopped her dead in her tracks. The monkey jumped down and scurried off down the street.

"I'm not through with you," she yelled as it disappeared out of sight, a blaring whistle bearing down on her. She turned to see a pink locomotive decorated in tulle and flowers pulled up beside her, and Stephen and Claire smiled down from the engine, their arms around one another. Then Stephen reached up and pulled the chain for the whistle.

Alex sat up with a start at the sound of the El roaring past her apartment, whistle blaring. Disoriented and nauseous, it took her a minute to realize where she was.

No monkey, no pink train. It was just a dream. But what the heck did it mean? Alex was a firm believer in dream interpretation, but she wasn't sure she wanted to know the symbolism behind the monkey on her back and the bridal train she was missing. Actually, she was pretty sure she knew what it meant. That only added to the pain that seemed to reach every one of her nerves.

She fell back on her pillows, the room spinning slightly as she tried to piece together the events of the night before. It was hard to stay focused with the rattle of the train and the pounding of her head, but she did seem to remember Peter bringing her home. She noted, peeking under the covers, she was neither naked nor in her clothes from last night, so she could be fairly certain nothing had happened.

Other than his actual presence in the apartment, she couldn't really recall a thing.

Lord only knows what I said to him, after the day I had.

She ticked off the events leading up to her evening, trying to determine when everything went a little hazy: the bridal fair, the closet, the security guard. The debutante who was planning the wedding of the year—Alex sat straight up again. The girl who was going to order enough invitations for Correspondence to be in the clear. Strangely, even with the thrilling prospect that her shop might soon be free and clear, all Alex could think about was her new savior in pearls.

Private school and a coming out party, etiquette lessons, she was sure Ashleigh had done them all. The right college, complete with a major that would allow her to be educated enough to sound intelligent. Nothing too scholastically challenging; she wouldn't want to appear bookish, nor would she be too distracted by her classes to miss the important events—the sorority galas and the fraternity formals.

Now, Ashleigh had found her perfect mate, a doctor who probably just wanted her to look proper and pretty and give a good dinner party. Alex wondered if they actually loved each other or if they just loved the idea of the life they would have.

Alex felt as though she was getting a look at what her mother had tried so hard to force on her. It made her stomach feel even worse.

A twinge of guilt surged inside her momentarily for being so judgmental of Ashleigh. Then Alex remembered the manicured fingers going to the strand of pearls at her neck.

Nope, that girl is going to get exactly what she wants in life, and easily, too. No reason to feel guilty, Alex reasoned as she rolled onto her back and stared up at the ceiling.

Having put the subject of Ashleigh to rest, she was confronted with the other lingering thought she had been doing her best to avoid—Peter.

But it wasn't just him that was troubling her. It was that suddenly she questioned the one thing she had always believed to be true—no good could come from a serious relationship. There seemed to be cracks forming in her theory.

Claire and Stephen had been so *normal* the night before. They were still themselves, even though they were so obviously together. Neither had changed at all. They didn't get all lovey-dovey and hang all over each other, nor did they point out each other's flaws as soon as the other left the table.

Hanging out with them last night had been just that—hanging out. Just like Valentine's Day had been with Peter, two people whose personalities seemed to complement each other.

She squeezed her eyes shut tight, willing the next thought not to come, but there it was—*Claire and Stephen are really into each other, maybe even in love with each other. So what does that say about me and Peter?*

"Aghhh!" She groaned loudly, throwing back the covers and climbing out of bed.

To her shock, the door to her room flew open. "Finally, you're awake! I was starting to think maybe you died in here or something!"

Claire stood in the open space wearing a pair of Alex's pajamas, all smiles. Alex was just about to reach out and strangle her when her bleary eyes caught sight of her saving grace, a grande cup from the Java Bean. Claire held it out to her, much like an animal trainer would do to a lion.

"Jeez, Claire, you scared the crap out of me," Alex said as she snatched the cup and held it to her nose to get a whiff. *Vanilla—there is a God.*

"I've been out there, waiting patiently to hear all about the rest of your night. I took Milo for a walk and got coffee, scones even. So shake the fog of your head and spill your guts! Peter was all smiles when I got here."

The words were like an artillery attack to Alex's throbbing head. She waved her hands for silence and walked into the bathroom for some aspirin, taking care to avoid catching her reflection in the mirror. That would only make her feel worse.

Claire had retreated to the couch in the living and sat there expectantly, scones and bottles of water spread in front of her on the coffee table. *She's good.*

Alex sat down next to her and took a drink of her coffee. "I don't actually remember much of last night, so if Peter was smiling, I wouldn't know why."

"Well, let's start from my arrival and work backward to the last thing you remember. Just focus on one thing at a time; that'll bring it back." It didn't take much for Claire to get her spy-girl thing going.

"All right." Alex was as anxious as Claire to find out what had happened. "What was I doing when you got here?"

"You were snoring on the couch," Claire said matter-of-factly.

"Snoring?" Alex was mortified. "What was Peter doing?"

"Getting ready to leave. He was glad I had come by because he was worried about locking the door behind him."

"He was leaving. That doesn't really sound promising. Why were you here?"

"You left your purse at the bar; you were in a big hurry to get out of there as soon as Peter showed up. You had your arms around him, and there were lipstick tracks around his mouth, so I'm pretty certain there was some kissing going on."

Alex stared at her blankly, trying to fix her mind on the night before. Though she couldn't remember exactly what happened, she could remember the feeling of being in Peter's arms, his mouth on hers. And most importantly, a sense of calm spreading through her as all of it went on.

"We did kiss, here and at the bar."

Claire's eyes danced. "So you do remember! Kissing, that's a good start."

Alex was amazed to find that she still felt that same calmness. All the panic she had felt just minutes earlier, lying in her bed trying to put a label on what was going on with Peter, what their connections meant—it was all gone, replaced by a serene, dare she say, happy feeling.

"I'm in love with Peter," she blurted.

"What?" Claire screamed so loud that Alex had to cover her ears. "You, the poster child for independence, are admitting, without protest, mind you, that you are *in love with Peter?*"

"I am. I am admitting it, because it's the truth. And, before you get so excited, this doesn't mean I'm not going to freak out. It just means I'm not going to freak out *right now*. I wonder if I told him," she pondered, sinking back into the pillows on the couch.

A flutter of nervousness passed through her, but she doused it with a sip from her coffee cup. In the state she had been in last night, who knew what she could have told him.

"Like I said, he was smiling when I got here, and he said that he could be very patient where you were concerned," Claire said, looking slightly amused. "I wasn't sure what he meant by that. At the time, I just assumed he was talking about you passing out. By the way, that's very admirable, not that I would expect any less from Peter. But still, some guys see a drunk woman as an easy target."

"Claire, you have got to stop talking so much." Alex rubbed at her temples. The aspirin was beginning to kick in, thankfully, but even without a hangover, Claire's rambling could give her a headache.

"So, how are you going to find out what you said to

him?" Claire leaned forward and picked up two scones from the table, handing one to Alex, who broke off a corner and popped it into her mouth.

"Call him, I guess?"

Claire nodded. "Yeah, you can drop some hints and see what he says. We should be able to figure it out from that."

"No, I don't want to play games with him. That's what I hate about the relationship thing. I'm just going to call him and tell him how I feel. I suppose that if he isn't surprised, then I probably told him last night, too."

Alex didn't feel spooked at all, and that made her squirm some. She needed to call before she realized what she was doing.

Claire sat with her mouth open, staring blankly at her. *This must be a first. I've silenced Claire.*

"What time is it? Is it too early to call him?" she said, ignoring the look on Claire's face completely.

She stood and went to check the clock in the kitchen, shocked to see that it was nearly noon. Yet another bit of evidence that she had over indulged the night before. Images of what she must have looked like flashed in her mind, and she wondered how foolish she had been. She was prone to fits of giggles that she couldn't control when she'd been drinking.

"You're calling, right now?" Claire had found her voice.

"Yep, before I start to realize how not me this is." Alex picked up the phone and slid down the wall to sit on the floor.

She dialed before she could think about it, and he answered before she could change her mind and hang up.

"Hello?" he answered, his voice so close to her ear that she felt her skin prickle.

All right, it's one thing to not be freaked out by all of this, but I refuse to be one of those giddy-in-love idiots who can't form a sentence. I might as well just be drunk all the time.

Alex cleared her throat. "Peter, it's Alex."

"How are you feeling this morning? Did you need me to make a house call?"

What did he mean by that? *Please God, tell me I didn't make any stupid let's-play-doctor jokes. Stay calm.*

"Actually, I'm feeling pretty good, though last night is a little bit fuzzy. I'm not quite sure where we left things."

Peter chuckled. "So you want me to let you off the hook for anything you might have said while under the influence?"

"No," Alex said quickly, her eyes darting to where Claire sat on the edge of the couch, waiting. "I, I, just wondered what I said last night. If I . . . if I told you . . ." She broke off, not sure how to continue.

Stammering, great, that's another check in the idiot column for those of you keeping track at home.

"Told me what?" The hint of teasing was gone from his voice now. He seemed to want to hear what she had to tell him as much as she wanted to say it.

Beep.

Darn call waiting.

Alex actually welcomed the chance to regain her composure before she continued.

"Peter, hold on one second, I've got another call."

From the daggers Claire was shooting her, it must be

some sort of bad relationship etiquette to answer the other line when you are declaring your feelings to the one you love for the first time.

She scowled right back at her and pushed the button on the phone. "Hello?"

"Ms. Sanders?" said a voice so proper Alex knew who it was immediately. "This is Ashleigh Rogers. I apologize for calling you at home, but I am going to need you to meet me at Correspondence this afternoon. It's the only time Mother can join me."

"Yes, well, Ms. Rogers, Correspondence isn't normally open on Sunday," Alex said, feeling utterly annoyed that this socialite would demand an appointment today.

"Perhaps you could make an exception for me," she replied with blatantly false sweetness. "I'm sure you can make an exception. Mother seems to think that we'll need close to a thousand invitations, and she is dying to get started."

Fake sweetness aside, that was a lot of invitations.

"Fine, I can meet you there at two," Alex said, trying to match Ashleigh's syrupy-sweet tone. She was, after all, a customer.

"Let's make it closer to one. I appreciate this more than you know. Ta-ta!"

She was gone before Alex could protest the change in time. *I am going to have to practically swallow my tongue to get through this.*

"Well, what's the deal?" Claire asked from the couch.

"I have to meet her in an hour. She's up to a thousand invitations, and she doesn't have a ring yet," Alex said. The reality of the order was suddenly clear. If this went through, it would save Correspondence by itself.

The thought of owning the store outright was overwhelming to her, and she let out a small hoot.

"She really is the answer to our prayers, even if she is the epitome of pathetic. I've known a lot of desperate women, but who actually plans their wedding before they've been asked?"

Claire shook her head. "Enough about Ashleigh, what did Peter say?"

"Crap. Peter. I forgot he was on the other line!" Alex clicked back over.

"Peter?"

"I'm still here. Now, I think you had something important to tell me." His voice was so warm and patient, Alex was almost distracted.

"I'm so sorry, but something big has come up at the shop and I have to get down there," she said tentatively. "It may just be the answer to all my problems. Can I call you later?"

It was just her luck that Ashleigh would call just as she was about to 'fess up to Peter about how she felt. He'd be totally in the right if he was annoyed with her, but he wasn't.

"That's great!" There was real excitement in his voice. "You can tell me about the shop then, and Alex, whenever you're ready to tell me the other thing, I'll be ready to hear it. Good luck today!"

Then he said good-bye, and Alex knew immediately that there was never going to be a reason to freak out about her feelings for Peter. Nope, just the sound of his voice calmed her, and that was as close to a perfect match as she was ever going to find.

Chapter Twenty-three

Peter smiled to himself as he placed the phone back on the charger. Even in the light of day, Alex was still willing to admit her feelings for him. It had crossed his mind that without her liquid courage from the night before, she might just try to dismiss what had happened, but her calling him this morning was a positive step. At least he chose to believe it was.

If he hadn't thought so before, now he knew—being with Alex was what he wanted more that anything. If that meant that starting his own practice would take longer then he planned, then it would. At least he'd have Alex in his life.

But it had also made him realize that trying to fix Ashleigh up with Michael was nothing more than a cop-out. If Alex could get past her fear of relationships, then he needed to do the same about his fears of losing his residency. If he lost his position because he broke up with Ashleigh, then so be it.

He glanced at his watch. He would call her, and

make plans for dinner. First, he had to work off some of the nervous energy he had built up thinking about Alex. The fresh air would do him some good, help him clear his thoughts and figure out the best way to break up with Ashleigh. It wouldn't be easy, but it had to be done.

It was the honorable thing to do. He was, after all, head over heels for another woman.

Alex flipped on the lights in the back of the shop. Besides her shower, this was her first moment of peace since Claire had burst into her room. It was a brief reprieve—Claire was coming for the meeting with Ashleigh after she had lunch with Stephen. Alex was glad she was coming. This one order could give her the money she needed, and she couldn't blow it by being rude to Ashleigh or her mother, no matter how annoying they were.

Alex knew from her experience with the social set that Ashleigh's mother was going to give her daughter a run for her money in the snob department. Alex had begged Claire to join them and bring refreshments. She would be the buffer they needed. Alex planned to kill them with kindness, or at least keep her mouth full so she couldn't insult them.

She flipped on some classical music—not what she would choose normally, but today it was all about the Rogers family. Then she started pulling out all her original invitations and setting them on the table. There were some beautiful things, most of which she had brought to the bridal fair, but one in particular Alex hadn't bothered to put in the portfolio because the materials were so expensive.

Now, she pulled it from the file and placed it in the middle of the table. It was exquisite, and she had a feeling Ashleigh was going to love it.

Alex had used a traditional Vladimir script in black on a crisp, white, refined cotton paper with a pale pink vellum overlay. It was elegant and unique, but traditional enough, she hoped, to impress Ashleigh's mother.

She was the real customer here, and Alex knew it. She was going to be the one writing the check.

Alex knew how to dabble in their world, as annoying as it was. She had been raised to belong there, spoke the language. This was her opportunity to break free of it for good. No matter what it took, she was going to make this sale.

The bells on the front door jingled her to attention. Alex slipped the invitation back into the file and took a deep breath before she turned to see Ashleigh and her mother standing just inside the front door of the store.

As she had suspected, they looked like the perfect mother-daughter pair, with matching highlights and manicured nails. The only difference Alex could see as she moved toward them, smiling, was that Ashleigh didn't have a giant diamond on her left hand as her mother did. If it weren't for the circumstances she'd found herself in, Alex would have loved to ask why.

Who plans a wedding without an engagement?

"Ashleigh, so good to see you," she said in a voice she hope sounded professional and sincere but thought probably sounded more stale and fake.

Neither of the Rogers women seemed to notice as they turned on their most polite smiles almost in unison. "Mother, this is Alex Sanders, the creative genius of the party invitation world."

Creative genius of the party invitation world? I get it; she needs to sell her mother on this as much as I do.

The thought stopped Alex dead in her tracks. This meant she and Ashleigh were playing on the same team. It took her utterly by surprise. Before she had time to decide if the development was good or bad, Claire came bustling in from outside, a coffee tray in one hand and a bag of pastries from the Corner Bakery held tightly in the other.

"Hello, ladies," she sang out. "Come in, let's get those coats off and get to work with planning the invitations to perfectly complement the most important day of your life!"

Alex stared after her as Claire walked past them all to the back of the store.

The best smile she could muster plastered on her face, Alex turned back around. Ashleigh was beaming, too. However, Mrs. Rogers looked less than thrilled to be planning the most important day of her daughter's life without the pesky detail of an engagement ring.

There is a certain poetic justice to this. A society wedding, the exact thing my mother threatened to close me down over, and their money will cut the cord from my parents for good. Bring it on, Mrs. Rogers.

"Yes, where are my manners? Please, let me take your coats and let's get to work." Her voice was even and clear, and she held her arms out to take their coats, giving Ashleigh a little wink to confirm their newfound sisterhood.

Then she ushered them to the back table, where

Claire had already poured the coffee into a carafe and put the pastries on a plate.

Alex smiled at her, but Claire was already in her wedding planning mode. All Alex had to do was sit back and watch Claire do her magic. Then, when she had wowed them with her ideas and the invitations before them, Alex could go in for the kill. She laid her hand on top of the folder and slid it closer.

"You must be Mrs. Rogers. I'm Claire, Alex's assistant. I help in the preliminary stages of your invitation experience."

Invitation experience? This was new.

Claire extended her hand to Ashleigh's mother, who shook it in that oh-so-proper way Alex was accustomed to, but it seemed to throw Claire a bit, because she was staring at the limp hand within her grasp.

"Coffee?" Alex asked, hoping to break the spell and snap Claire back into reality.

"Yes, please," Mrs. Rogers replied, pulling her hand back. "I'm not sure what my daughter has told you about her plans. Let's start there." Her voice was refined, showing no emotion.

Ashleigh sat next to her mother, smiling meekly. Gone was the assertive woman she had been at the bridal fair and on the phone earlier in the day.

"Well, from what I understand, her *impending* engagement will set the stage for the wedding of the season. She thought it would be a good idea for the two of you to get a jump on things to help the planning go smoothly." Alex surprised even herself with this little speech.

"So this is just a little preliminary shopping trip." This last part did the trick, as the word *preliminary* seemed to calm Mrs. Rogers's nerves, and the rest of them relaxed.

Alex nodded at Claire, who pulled out the first of their custom invitations and began to go over the options. Mrs. Rogers asked all the appropriate questions about color and font style, engraving and printing, even if there were coordinating thank-you notes available.

By the time they had reached the third invitation, Alex knew she had her. Even Ashleigh was chiming in here and there; all Alex had to do was wait them out.

An hour into it, they had begun to sort what they were seeing into piles of yes, maybe, and definitely not. They were even giggling and laughing.

"Now, this is the one you really liked yesterday," Alex said, handing Ashleigh the homemade paper with inlaid rose petals. They were down to the last choice before the folder.

"Yes, this is so beautiful. What do you think of it, Mother?" Ashleigh laid the card in front of her and looked at her with great anticipation.

"Well, it is unique," Mrs. Rogers began. "But I'm not sure it expresses the formality of the occasion. I mean, you are the *daughter* of a doctor, *marrying* a doctor. And it is a bit feminine; I don't know if either of the men in our lives would approve."

It was a far cry from the Mrs. Rogers who had come through the door an hour earlier. She was ripe for the buy, and Alex was ready and waiting for her.

"Well, there is one more I can show you. It's a great combination of all the things you are looking for." She pulled it out of the folder and laid it on the table in front of them.

Their eyes grew large as they both looked at the invitation.

"This is exquisite," Mrs. Rogers murmured.

"The pink is so me," Ashleigh practically squealed.

Alex caught Claire's eye above the table and smiled. An invitation they had created had reduced Ashleigh from a well-bred young woman into a squealing teenager.

"This is it. This is the one we want." She tapped the table next to the card. "Now that just leaves us with one important detail to discuss," Mrs. Rogers said evenly.

"Yes, well, we can go over pricing if you can just give us an estimate as to how many invitations you might need," Alex replied, trying hard to keep a handle on her growing excitement.

A high-pitched laugh escaped Mrs. Rogers's mouth as she titled her head to the side and looked Alex square in the eye.

"No, this isn't about *cost*. I need to be sure that no one else has used this invitation before Ashleigh, and that no one will after."

Game, set, and match. Correspondence is all but mine.

"I assure you, we haven't sold this invitation to any-one. And as soon as we have your deposit, I will guar-antee you that I won't even show it to anyone else."

"Then you, my dear, have yourself a deal." She held out her hand and shook it in the same manner she had done with Claire, but it didn't phase Alex one bit.

She made her own hand go as limp as that of the woman across the table.

"All right," Claire chimed in. "Now that we have a style picked out, let's work on the wording."

Alex left them at the table. This was Claire's area of expertise, and she didn't need Alex hanging over her shoulder while she worked.

She sat down behind her desk and tried to make herself look busy and important while her mind plotted the exact moment she could announce to her parents that she no longer needed their help. She was really an independent woman, or would be as soon as she got that deposit check—a stroke of genius on her part, really.

It had come to her while she was talking. Just the threat of someone else getting the perfect invitation, Alex knew, would be enough to get Mrs. Rogers to write a check that day.

Now they were back there going over the details, and she was so giddy she couldn't focus on anything but the fact that she had reached her goal.

The ring of a cell phone snapped her back into reality. Ashleigh squealed, "It's him!" and then answered the phone. "Hello, darling," she purred.

Alex caught Claire's eye over the Rogers' heads and rolled her eyes. Claire shot her a look, but couldn't hide her disgust as Ashleigh continued to use the sickeningly sweet voice in what, thankfully, was a very brief conversation.

"He wants to meet me for dinner tonight. He says he has something important to talk to me about!" Ashleigh gushed. "I can't wait to tell him all about this. Are we almost through?"

"Yes, yes, I just need to write the deposit check then we can scoot along and get you all beautiful for your big night."

This time it was Claire's turn to roll her eyes at Alex, who shot her a look. They were about to be paid.

Mrs. Rogers wrote out a check and handed it to Claire. "As you heard, we need to hurry along, so I'll fax over the information you requested—names and locations, right? I'm sure that check will more than hold our invitation." Claire nodded, her mouth hanging open a bit.

"We'll be in touch with further details," Ashleigh chimed in, her voice full of the cold confidence she had displayed earlier in the day. With that, the two of them pulled on their coats and floated out of Correspondence.

Claire trailed behind them and laid the check in front of Alex, who was about to say how sick it was that a call from a man could send grown women scurrying. Until, that is, her eye caught sight of all the zeros on the check in front of her.

Chapter Twenty-four

As soon as she had managed to process the amount of the check, Alex grabbed the phone and dialed Stephen's cell.

"Hello," he answered, and Alex, unable to keep a handle on her excitement, cut him off.

"Stephen, I have the money for the down payment in my hand! Call and make the offer right now, before we lose the building!"

"Alex, hold on—you're telling me that Ashleigh woman paid in advance?"

Alex flapped her hand up and down, the reality of it overwhelming her. "Something like that. It's a long story, but the bottom line is, I have the money, make the offer!"

After going over the details, amounts, and the like, they hung up. By the end, Stephen was as excited as she was.

Spurred on, Alex and Claire spent the remainder of the day inside the closed store, making contact with the brides-to-be they had met the day before. Their objective was to set up appointments with as many of them as they could, strike while the iron was hot.

Alex could feel her excitement building with each phone call, since more were making appointments than weren't. Looking at the list of bookings in front of her, Alex was sure even without Ashleigh, she would have been able to save her store.

But that was beside the point, because she had Ashleigh, and soon she would have the building. More important, she would have her independence. Alex could soon stand on her own, without her father's money or having to hear her mother's constant nagging about her love life.

My love life, she thought, as she crossed the last name off her list. She and Peter would drop the charade of being together. Though she was sure about her feelings for him, doubt lingered in her subconscious that she was anything more than a community service project for him. But she pushed those doubts aside and instead focused on what it had felt like to kiss him the night before.

"Alex, oh Alex," a singsong voice from somewhere else called to her, and she realized she had been gazing blindly out the window, reliving the night before.

The smell of Peter, the feel of him, even the taste of him, the details of their evening becoming clearer to her as the day went on.

She forced her attention to the present. In front of her sat Claire, arms crossed and waiting, apparently, for Alex to snap out of it.

"Hey, Claire." Startled, Alex shuffled through the papers on her desk, embarrassed at having been caught in a daydream. The way Claire was looking at her, it was almost as if she knew exactly what Alex had been thinking.

"I don't need to ask where your head was. You're starting to develop an actual 'Peter look,'" Claire giggled. To her surprise, Alex couldn't protest; she only blushed, because she knew Claire was right.

"It's pretty amazing that one man could change the way you have thought about the entire gender for so many years. I guess you really do just have to find the right person," Claire continued, her voice trailing off as she walked toward the back of the store. She sat at the table still covered in wedding invitations and began to straighten up, humming a snappy little tune as she worked.

Something about Claire was different, Alex noted. It was more than just Alex admitting her feeling for Peter. No, something was definitely up with Claire.

Maybe it's this wedding talk. It must be going to her head.

"So, Stephen didn't mind shortening your lunch date?" Alex fished. It still seemed so strange to her that the two of them had become a couple and she hadn't even noticed.

"Nope, he was fine with it." Something in her voice told Alex there was more to it. She stood and walked around the desk to where her best friend sat.

"All right, you can be as coy as you want, but I know something is going on." Her voice was firm. "So you can just tell me now, Claire."

She sat down in the chair opposite her, trying to do her best impersonation of the security guard at the bridal fair, but she couldn't hold a straight face.

Claire met her grin; it seemed as though the two of them could do nothing but smile at each other all day long.

"You caught me; I didn't want to bring it up, really. But Stephen brought up marriage, and not just in an obscure reference. He was talking about us!"

Alex stared at her blankly. All the talk of marriage and invitations and feelings were one thing, but marriage for Stephen and Claire was another thing all together. She had barely gotten used to the idea that they were dating.

"It's a bit early for *that* kind of discussion, isn't it?" she said, reaching for a leftover pastry from the plate on the table. She focused on picking at the stale outer layer while she waited for Claire to answer.

"Early for you, maybe, but Stephen and I have been together for a while now," Claire said matter-of-factly. She lifted her gaze from the invitations in front of her to Alex's face across the table.

"A while? What's it been, Claire—one month? Maybe two? I just don't know how you can have such a conversation so soon."

A surge of guilt hit Alex hard. Saving Correspondence had been all she'd thought about. It hadn't crossed her mind that all this matrimony talk might send her wedding-obsessed friend around the bend.

Claire looked right at Alex as she spoke, her voice deliberate, but not angry. "He brought it up, not me. Honestly, this is the first relationship I have ever had in which I didn't spend most of the time planning the future. With Stephen, the present is good enough." As she spoke, her whole face lit up. Alex was stunned.

As long as she had known Claire, it had always been

about getting married. Every guy she saw, every date she went on—all she focused on was what he would look like at the end of the aisle.

Just another shocker in a day that was full of them.

"He didn't propose. We were just talking about marriage. Besides, even if we've only been dating a few months, we've been friends for a few years," she quipped. "I even tried to help him pick up that counter girl at the Java Bean. Oh, that was the other thing. You should have seen the look on her face when he kissed me today. She really did think he was gay."

Claire's eyes grew to emphasize her astonishment, and with that, the serious talk was over. They erupted into giggles at the memory of that girl introducing Stephen to her brother. It really had been a strange few months, for all of them.

"Can you believe that this all started the night you met Peter?"

"It did, didn't it? I had forgotten that; it's all been a bit of a blur since that dinner with my dad. Peter just seemed to get rolled up into the drama of it. Kind of like you." Alex paused. "You know, Claire, I can't thank you enough for all of your help with this. I could never have done this without you."

"Are you talking about the store, or Peter?" Claire's eyes danced.

"I was talking about the store, but Peter, too," Alex replied, trying to find the words to describe her feelings. "You and Stephen and the way you are with each other, it showed me that not all relationships are horrible, like my parents'. It made me trust my feelings for Peter. Hopefully when I tell him, he'll feel the same way."

Claire nodded in agreement, a silly grin on her face. "A relationship of mine seen as a role model. Now who would ever have thought that?"

"Not me." Alex found her sarcasm again. "If you'll excuse me, I need to make just one more call."

She stood and walked back to her desk. Picking up the phone, she punched the number she knew by heart, then sat down behind her desk and waited for an answer.

"Dad, it's Alex," she said when he picked up. "I need to meet with you as soon as possible."

As she waited for his answer, she picked up Mrs. Rogers's check. Flipping it over, she endorsed the back, writing "for deposit only" beneath the black script of her signature.

"Yes, the club for lunch tomorrow will be fine. I'll see you there," she said, flipping the check back over and counting the zeros once again.

"And Dad, drinks are on me," she added before she hung up, sharing a smile with Claire. When she was done with her dad, she'd give Peter a call, and with any hope, soon she would have everything she'd ever wanted.

Peter took a deep breath and let it out slowly. There was no turning back now. Ashleigh was walking across the restaurant toward him, and he could tell by the look on her face that she had no idea what he wanted to talk to her about. He wasn't sure if that made it better or worse. At least she wouldn't have a scripted response to all of his reasons for ending things. She wasn't going to take it well. That he knew for sure.

Ashleigh Rogers had never been broken up with in her life. Until tonight, that is.

"Peter, darling," she cooed as he rose to help her with her chair. She leaned forward to kiss him and he turned his face just in time. Her freshly applied lipstick left its impression on his cheek instead of on his mouth, where she had intended it to go.

A puzzled look crossed her face, and he smiled grimly at her as he sat back down across from her.

"This is a quaint place," she said, scrunching up her nose and looking around.

"Quaint," in Ashleigh speak, meant that for one reason or another she did not approve.

Peter glanced around the small space. Burgundy curtains hung in the windows, and half-melted candles stuck in wine bottles sat in the middle of tables covered in the same color. The smell of garlic and other fragrant spices permeated the air. He had chosen it because of its proximity to the hospital, but the food was good, too.

Ashleigh reached across the table and grabbed his hand. "I suppose the place doesn't matter, just us. I have some wonderful news to tell you."

Peter wondered briefly what could have her so excited. Probably one of her other friends had gotten engaged or maybe broken up? That would mean she wasn't the last single girl on the planet.

"Ashleigh, I have something I need to talk to you about." He hoped the use of her name would get her attention. However, the dreamy look in her eyes remained.

The waiter came, a thin young man with blond hair and multiple earrings. Peter felt the hot, flushed feeling he always got when Ashleigh talked to waiters. Her superiority mixed with an insincere gratitude, as though this waiter couldn't possibly know the particular wine she wanted.

Peter smiled in an apologetic way as he ordered a club soda with lime. Ashleigh's face fell.

"You're not drinking. Does that mean you're on call?" Her voice sounded like that of a neglected child, and Peter bristled.

"In a few hours." Again, he wondered how she could think of nothing but a future as a doctor's wife and be so clueless about the hours a doctor had to work. Her own father worked similar hours.

"I thought, when you said you had something to tell me, that it would be an all-night thing." The smile was gone from her face now.

It dawned on him then, what she was expecting. The realization hit him in the pit of the stomach. He was about to break up with her on the very night that she was expecting a proposal.

He swallowed hard and wished he could drink.

They sat there in a moment of uncomfortable silence, not looking at each other.

"We need to talk about us," he began, looking across the table at Ashleigh's wide blue eyes, glistening with anticipation.

"I don't think we're going in the same direction." A veil seemed to fall over her eyes, and her mouth pinched itself tightly together. Noting her still silence, he continued.

"What I'm trying to say—though not very well, I admit—is that you are a great girl and I've been lucky to have this time with you. But I've come to realize we don't have enough in common to make this work long term." He paused and looked her in the eye.

"And you deserve a man who sees the same future ahead of him that you do. That man is not me, and I think if you really think about it, you'll agree." He hoped that she would hear the earnest tone of his voice and understand he was doing this as much for her as he was for himself.

"You're breaking up with me?" Her voice was incredulous. "All I've done for you, all my father has done for you, and you're ending this, tonight?" She shook her head in disbelief.

"You can't be that surprised. I've told you before that my dream is to have a small practice, live a quiet life. You want a man whose ambitions are greater than that. You know that's not me."

He felt a calm spread through him that he hadn't felt in a long time. It didn't matter what she said, or what happened to him next. This was the right thing to do.

"What is my mother going to say?" she said in disbelief, a look of slight terror in her eyes.

Peter smiled grimly. Of course, that would be her first thought. Her mother.

"She'll see it, too. You and I are not right for each other . . ."

"And my father," she interrupted, her eyes blazing now. "He picked you for chief resident, to follow in his footsteps as his future son-in-law." She shook her head in disbelief as the waiter approached their table with menus.

Peter waved him off, hoping his smile was enough of an apology. They weren't going to be needing menus tonight.

"I'm not the same kind of doctor as your father, not the same kind of man he is. He's said as much to me before."

Ashleigh glared at him, the weight of her feelings—whether true anger or humiliation, he wasn't sure—written on her face.

"You're not even close to the kind of man he is! You have no ambition, no drive. All I've done for you, teaching you about culture and society, and you are throwing it all away!"

She was yelling, and as much as he felt it was her right to be angry, he wasn't about to be humiliated.

"Ashleigh, whether you want to admit it or not, your father wouldn't have given me that job if I weren't a competent doctor." He paused before he spoke again, his voice low. "And, for the record, in all the time we have been together, only you have mentioned marriage. I hoped you would see the plain truth when I spoke it. You and I just weren't meant for each other. We're two different people."

Ashleigh stood abruptly, picked up her water glass. "I've wasted enough of my time with a loser like you," she fumed, and then threw the contents in his face. "You'll never be anything more than some small-time doctor. I'm better than that." With that, she slammed the glass down on the table, grabbed her purse and coat, and stormed from the restaurant, leaving Peter wet and alone with all eyes on him.

"Exactly what I was trying to say," he said to himself, smiling. "I am just a small-time doctor."

Chapter Twenty-five

The waiter set their menus on the table. "Anyone care for a drink?" Alex briefly considered ordering champagne, but that would have been too obvious, not to mention that it lacked a certain air of professionalism. That was what she was going for—the hope that finally her father would see her as a professional.

"I'll take a scotch on the rocks, and my daughter will have a martini."

Stephen had called the night before. Mrs. Thompson had gladly accepted her offer, saying something like she couldn't wait to tell Mr. Thompson that she had sold his tax shelter right out from under his cheating nose. Alex had been so happy, she had even managed to ignore her normal impulse to curse marriage.

They had met that morning—honoring Mrs. Thompson's request that the deal be quick and kept quiet. The older woman had signed the agreement with a flourish, cackling to herself that she was sticking it to her husband. Alex had signed, too, and her enthusiasm was equal to the seller's, though for different reasons, of course.

Now was her real moment of truth. Sitting across from her father, she was the picture of poise on the outside. However, her mind still buzzed with anticipation.

"So, Alex, what is this all about?" he asked as he picked up his menu.

Alex smiled at him. "Well, Dad, the last time we were here, you issued me an ultimatum. We need to follow up on that."

She wanted to draw this out a bit, and enjoy her success. It gave her a feeling of freedom she had never known before. To be free of obligation to her parents was something new.

"I thought we had already reached an agreement. You took my advice and started seeing Peter, your mother backed down, and everything is proceeding as usual, just as it should be." He winked at her and leaned back in his chair.

As it should be. Alex's eyes widened in surprise at the comment. Did her father really enjoy his control over her that much? She had taken him for the softer of her parents. His condescending tone sounded much like her mother's, as if Alex couldn't possibly think for herself. It made her feel like a teenager, and her temper boiled beneath the surface in frustration. Just as it always seemed to be, where one of her parents was concerned.

She took a drink of her martini. She was in control of this meeting, even if he didn't realize it.

He was about to.

"Well, the terms of *that* agreement didn't suit me, so I went ahead"—she paused and met his glance evenly—"and bought the building." She reached into her purse and pulled out the real estate contract, laying it on the table in front of him. Then she leaned back in her chair and winked at him.

It took him a moment—she could tell by the confused look on his face—to realize what it meant. He picked it up and inspected it closely.

"Well, I guess this is the end of our business relationship," he said matter-of-factly. His face didn't betray any emotion, if he felt anything at all.

Alex was stunned. She didn't really know how this was going to play out, but simple contrition on his part was not what she had anticipated.

"That's it? 'End of our business relationship,' that's all you can come up with?"

He met her gaze. "Well, yes. You don't need me to negotiate a lease or rent you a space anymore, so that's the end of things. Isn't that what you wanted?"

Until now, she had thought it was. All the work she had done these last few months, it was all to get to this moment, to cut the ties to her father's business. But now as she sat here, she realized it wasn't what she wanted at all. The turnaround from just a few moments ago made her head spin. She wasn't used to her emotions clouding her perspective.

As she looked across the table at her father, it struck her for the first time how much she wanted his respect and his affection.

"I thought it was. But now, I realize, I want something else," she said quietly.

The lines around his eyes softened. "And what is that, Alex?"

Alex looked around the restaurant, the waiters moving about the room with trays of food or drinks. There were tables of people talking and laughing with one another. Different groupings of relationships, that's what they were. Just like in the days following her first encounter with Peter, when everywhere she looked, there were couples—here, everywhere her eyes stopped, she could see relationships. It was obvious to her for the first time that she'd spent so much of her adult life trying to get away from her parents that she'd never realized how much she wanted to be with them.

"I want to still have our monthly dinners," she said softly, hoping that he understood what she was trying to say.

The serious look on his face gave way to a small smile. "I would like that, very much. And Alex, I want something from you, too."

"What is it?" she said, gripping the arms of her leather chair, unsure of what he might say next. They were in new territory now.

"Well, first let me say that I know your mother and I were never really the greatest role models for you where marriage was concerned."

She arched an eyebrow. "I learned a great deal from the two of you." Alex had no idea what he might say next. They were in such a good place at this moment, and she didn't want it ruined.

"Well, I can only imagine what those things might be, but what I want you to understand is . . . there was another side of us you never saw. Our marriage, though fiery at times, has some bright spots, too. Maybe we wouldn't have stayed together otherwise."

Alex's mind was full of reasons—*social standing, custody of their box seats at the opera,* the list went on and on.

"So what does any of that have to do with me?"

He leaned forward, his green eyes wide. "Well, I just worry that you may not be willing to dive into your own relationship, because of us." He leaned back and sighed. "I'm not trying to sound like your mother and pry into your personal life. What I'm saying is"—he paused— "you shouldn't try so hard to be independent, because it would sure be a shame if you ended up alone."

How many surprises am I supposed to deal with in one day?

Alex looked around for either a hidden camera or her mother with a straitjacket for her. Relationship advice from her father was beyond her realm of comprehension.

Her mouth hung open in surprise, and he leaped on her silence to land the final shocking blow.

"You see, all the bickering and fighting between your mother and me is just another expression of our passion for each other."

Alex squeezed her eyes tight, trying to block out any kind of mental picture that might come with that last remark. She held her hand up to try to stop him from continuing.

"I get it, Dad." She looked around for the waiter. She might need another drink for this conversation to continue.

However, there may not be enough liquor in the free world for this conversation.

Her father's face turned beet red. "That wasn't what I was trying to say."

"That's comforting."

"Honestly, Alex," he said, finding his fatherly tone of voice. "Peter seems like a great guy. Give him a chance. That's all I'm trying to say. End of subject."

"Good," Alex said, smiling. Peter's name brought her newfound feelings for him to the surface. She could feel the smile spread from her mouth to her eyes, until she felt like she might actually be radiating.

"He is a very nice man," she said, unable to explain herself any other way.

"So, how'd you do it?" he asked, steering the subject away from her love life. "How'd you get Thompson to sell to you? Maybe I can learn a thing or two about business from you."

He tried to sound mocking, but the look on his face was one of pure pride, and Alex could feel her smile deepen until her cheeks actually hurt.

Of all the surprises she had had that day, her father's pride in her was the cherry on the top. And, like her feelings for Peter, she hadn't realized how good it would feel to just admit it.

As soon as she finished telling her father the details of her business coup, she was going to set the stage for one in her personal life as well. Peter wasn't going to know what hit him.

Chapter Twenty-six

Alex felt like she was floating on air as she walked back to Correspondence. In typical Chicago fashion, just when it seemed as though winter would never end, a perfect day came along. The sun was shining, the sky was a brilliant blue. There was warmth in the air that foretold an eventual end to what always seemed like neverending winter.

The mood Alex was in, there could have been a raging blizzard and she wouldn't have noticed. She'd been smiling so much since lunch with her father that her cheeks ached. To add to her giddiness, she'd made a date with Peter for that evening. As she thought of it, she could feel her grin deepen to the point that anyone she passed on the street might believe her to be either medicated or delirious.

Something about his voice had been different, like he was relieved or something. He had something to tell her, too, he said in the few moments they had on the phone that morning before her meeting. Alex hoped it had something to do with their brief conversation the morning before—that he was in love with her.

He wouldn't have to wait much longer to tell her whatever it was. Alex only had to get through the day and then, for the first time in her life, she could tell a man she was in love with him.

Yes, it had been a wonderful but strange few days, and as she crossed the street, she wondered what surprises the afternoon might have in store for her. They were booked solid with the bridal appointments she and Claire had set up. It would be busy, that was for sure, but it suited Alex just fine. After lunch with her father, she felt surer of herself as a businesswoman then ever before.

As she reached Correspondence, she paused in front of it to drink it all in. It was hers, outright. The displays in the window, the smudges on the front door—all of it belonged to her. She ran her fingers over the hand-painted logo on the door and felt a sense of pride. Her smile deepened, if that was even possible. Life somehow had become picture-perfect. And the biggest shock of all was she didn't want to pack her bags and run off to New Zealand to escape her newly formed relationships. Nope, all of it seemed to fit just fine.

"Alex." The voice snapped her back to reality, and she turned to see Stephen, a serious look on his face.

"Stephen," she practically sang out, but his face didn't change. A look of nervousness flashed in his eyes, and he let out a big sigh.

Dial it down a notch, Alex.

Obviously, something was bothering Stephen. Alex felt a wave of guilt. It had been a while since any of them had talked about anything but saving the store . . .

and Peter. It made her realize how self-involved she'd been during the last few months. It also made her feel guilty; none of her success could have happened without Stephen or Claire.

"Everything all right, Stephen?" Alex asked brightly—but not too brightly, she hoped.

"Hmmph," was all Stephen replied, handing her one of the paper cups in his hand.

Alex looked at him quizzically. "Coffee in the afternoon? Seriously, what's going on?"

He stared at her blankly, and then ran his fingers through his hair. "We'll get to it. First, I want you to tell me about lunch with your dad."

"No, no, no. That's all we've talked about for the last few months. *My* business, *my* father, heck, even *my* love life, which as you know is uncharted territory. It's all fine. It's all good. Now I want you to tell me what's bothering *you*." She raised her eyebrows to tell him she meant it. But before he could answer, Claire came bursting out of the store.

"Alex, thank goodness you're here! I need to run and get some paper for the fax—you won't believe it when you see—there was paper everywhere when I got in! I'll be right back, and then you can tell me all about lunch!" She smiled at Stephen, then kissed him on the cheek before hurrying up the street. Alex turned, ready to put the full court press to him, but found he had already walked inside.

If her clumsiness was contagious, maybe her insanity was, too, she thought as she followed him.

Stephen stopped at her desk and picked up a page from the large stack that sat there.

She followed his glance to where the fax machine sat behind the desk, blinking like some sort of short-circuited robot. The entire ream of paper was gone from the paper tray.

Turning, he smiled at Alex. "Saying your business is good might be the understatement of the year," he said, handing her the paper.

Her eyes skimmed it quickly. It was the specifics of a wedding order. Bride, groom, date—all the details. Claire had asked their appointments to fax them over so they could get a jump on the orders. Alex flipped through the first few on the pile, scanning the specifics as she did. She recognized some of the names from the bridal fair. Images of their young faces flashed in her mind. She wondered again how many of them were planning the wedding while giving no thought to the actual marriage.

Apparently, her newfound faith in relationships hadn't squashed all of her anxiety about the bond of holy matrimony.

"Jeez, Claire told me the orders were rolling in, but I had no idea," Stephen said, sipping his coffee.

"Yeah, it looks like we have our work cut out for us today," Alex said, trying to put a lid on her anxiety. "But before I dive into this, you need to tell me what has you so worked up."

She set the paper back on the stack, crossed her arms in front of her, and looked him dead in the eye.

Stephen smiled sheepishly, stuck his hand in his pocket, pulled out a tiny box, and shoved it toward her. "This."

Alex took the box and opened it to reveal a bright, shiny engagement ring.

Alex felt all the blood run out of her face as she looked at the ring.

Were they all trying to kill her? *Just because I've managed to fall in love with Peter and see some good in my parents' marriage doesn't mean I can process all this marriage instantly!*

She took a big sip of the coffee in her hand and tried to get her bearings. Then, like an epiphany from above, or maybe a jolt of caffeine—she couldn't be sure which—she felt herself relax. Hadn't Claire and Stephen's relationship been the whole reason she had been willing to admit her feelings for Peter? It was just her instinct to object to marriage, on principle.

That was the Alex of old; the new and improved version could be happy for her friends. However, she still had her doubts about the fifty or so brides who had faxed her the night before.

"Stephen, it's beautiful," she said sincerely, handing it back to him. "Claire is going to lose her mind over it."

"Over what?" Claire's voice sang out from the front of the store. Alex and Stephen both turned to face her, startled that she had appeared.

"All these orders," Alex stammered, stepping in front of Stephen so he could put the ring back in his pocket. "We've got a busy afternoon in front of us." Her voice sounded strange even to her, and Claire tilted her head and narrowed her eyes inquisitively.

Stephen stepped around Alex quickly. "Yep, so I will get out of your hair." He reached Claire and took her in his arms, wiping the confusion from her face with a kiss. "I'll stop back after work and we'll get dinner." He kissed her again and walked out the door.

"Try to stay focused, Alex," he called over his shoulder as the door swung shut. Claire's look of confusion returned, and Alex picked up some of the papers and shrugged her shoulders.

Peter paused outside the door of Dr. Rogers's office. He had decided the best way to deal with the fallout of his break-up was to confront it. He had broken up with Ashleigh because he wanted to save her from heartbreak in the end. It wasn't as though her father was thrilled with him as a prospective son-in-law, anyway. Dr. Rogers should be happy with this turn of events.

As many times as he tried to convince himself that his boss would greet the end of his relationship warmly, he knew the reality of it was the opposite. Images of a hysterical Ashleigh demanding her father fire Peter for breaking her heart had plagued Peter as soon as he'd gotten to the hospital. So, instead of lingering in the halls waiting for his summons, here he was, smiling anxiously at Dr. Rogers's secretary, waiting to plead his case.

Tonight he was going to have to tell Alex about Ashleigh, he knew. He wasn't sure how the news of his ex-girlfriend was going to sit with Alex. He hoped that when he explained the situation, his job, Ashleigh's connection to it, how he felt trapped by his circumstances, Alex would understand. If not, then he hoped the fact that he was head over heels in love with her would be enough to salvage their relationship.

Before he could answer that question, Dr. Rogers's door swung open, and Peter looked up to see Michael standing in the doorway. Dr. Rogers stood behind him, a smile on his face as he shook Michael's hand and patted him on the back.

Peter felt his stomach fall.

"Thank you for coming in, Dr. Harris," the chief of staff said. "We'll discuss the details when the papers are in order. And let me again thank you for your help with the situation last night."

Last night? What situation could Michael have been helpful in last night? Peter could think of only one involving the Rogers family the night before.

"Glad I could be there to help," Michael said, exiting the office, "and I am the one that should be thanking you, sir."

Dr. Rogers just smiled and thumped him on the back again, then he seemed to notice Peter standing there and his look of happiness melted into a tight-lipped smile. "I'll be in touch," he said, his tone indicating that he was done with Michael.

"I look forward to it," Michael said. As he passed Peter, he smiled and winked. Peter barely had time to compose himself before Dr. Rogers stepped out of the door and called for him to come in.

Peter closed the door behind him and stood anxiously in front of the chair where just weeks ago, he had been promoted. Ashleigh's face looked down from the wall.

This is not the way this was supposed to go.

He took a deep breath and forged ahead. "Dr. Rogers, I just want to say how sorry I am that things didn't work out between Ashleigh and me," he began.

Dr. Rogers lifted his hands from his desk and with one flick of his finger, cut Peter off.

"Dr. Gibson, let me begin by saying I thought I made myself pretty clear the last time we met."

"Yes, perfectly clear, sir, but if you'd let me explain . . ."

"I think you explained yourself pretty clearly to Ashleigh last night. Now if you would take a seat, I will continue." His eyes looked across the desk intently at Peter. Not knowing what else to do, Peter sank into the chair behind him and awaited his inevitable dismissal.

"Now that I have your attention, I would like to thank you." He paused as Peter nearly choked in surprise.

"Thank me for what?" he stammered.

"Showing my daughter what I had been telling her all along. That the two of you were not suited for one another."

Though his tone was sharp, it didn't seem to Peter that Dr. Rogers was angry in the least bit. In fact, he seemed almost smug.

Peter was speechless.

"You see, her mother and I have raised her with a certain level of expectation for her future. I knew from the first time I worked with you, you would never be able to provide that for her. However, she wouldn't hear of it." He glanced at Peter over his metal frames. "You were like her little project. She was determined to prove me wrong, but last night, she finally saw what I had been saying all along." He smiled knowingly at Peter. "And for that, I thank you."

"Dr. Rogers, I'm going to be honest here. I'm not sure what it is you want me to say. Your daughter, as you know, is a wonderful girl, and I'm sure she will find someone that you all can agree on." Peter glanced across the desk, and was shocked to see a wide smile greeting him.

"I believe she already has. You see, last night she came here to find me after your dinner, and she ran into Michael. He was very kind and comforted her. He even brought her home, and from what I gather, the two of them instantly recognized what I have known for months. They have a great deal in common."

Peter was surprised and relieved that Ashleigh had found some comfort the night before, but the writing was on the wall.

"I assume that Dr. Harris will be the new chief ER resident?" Peter said, resigned to his fate.

"Actually, no."

Even as he heard them spoken, the words didn't quite register with Peter. *No?*

"It turns out that Michael is more interested in pursuing a specialty in surgery, so unless you have reason to resign your position, I'd like you to remain chief resident in the ER."

It seemed impossible to Peter that this whole episode was going to turn out so well. There had to be some sort of catch.

"But you said if I broke Ashleigh's heart you'd not only fire me, you'd make sure I couldn't find a job at any hospital in the city," he said incredulously.

"Ah, but you didn't break her heart, did you? By breaking up with her, you pushed her right into Michael's arms. She's never been happier. Besides, all the reports I get from the ER show that it's running better than it has in years. As long as that continues, the job is yours. We both know that there is no reason it shouldn't be your top priority."

Julie Stone

Peter was bright enough to get the implication. He had no girlfriend, so there wasn't anything to take precedence over his work.

It could be worse. Peter shook his head and chuckled at how blind he had been. Dr. Rogers had probably planned on this happening all along. If he wasn't so relieved, he'd feel a bit used, but what was the point? He was free of Ashleigh, still had his job, and tonight . . . he was finally going to get together with Alex.

"I think it's I who should thank you," Peter said, standing and extending his hand. "I'm not exactly sure how it happened, but I think we both just got what we wanted."

Chapter Twenty-seven

T he store was quiet—dark and quiet, actually. Just the occasional sound of a passing car broke the silence. Alex sat at her desk, staring at the piece of paper in front of her. The only light, aside from the ones in the front windows, was from the single lamp on her desk. Claire was gone, off getting engaged to a beaming Stephen. Alex was glad she had been alone when she came across the fax.

She and Claire had been busy the rest of the day, but they'd both felt on top of the world, shooting each other knowing smiles across the heads of regular customers and wedding appointments.

When Stephen had appeared with flowers at the end of the day, he handed the bouquet to a surprised Alex, pulling just one pale pink rose out and handing it to Claire.

"Congratulations on the store and everything else," he said. Then he turned his attention to Claire, his eyes sparkling. "You and I are going bowling!"

To Alex's surprise, Claire squealed with delight.

Alex had never taken either of them for bowlers, but who could explain what love did to people? She had wished them a fabulous evening and sent them on their way, locking the door behind them. She had just a short while to wait before her own date arrived. Enough time to get the place cleaned up.

That was when she had found it, as she was straightening up—a single stray slip of paper that had fallen under the cart where the fax sat finally silent.

"Now, which lucky wannabe-bride do you belong to?" she muttered to herself as she flipped it over. The words hit her like a punch in the stomach.

Dr. and Mrs. William Rogers
Request the honor of your presence
At the wedding
Of their daughter
Ashleigh Therese
To
Dr. Peter Gibson

There was more, but Alex couldn't bring herself to read it. *Peter* was the doctor Ashleigh wanted to marry? Her Peter?

It was almost too much for Alex to wrap her mind around. She had been so sure Peter felt the same way about her that she did about him. Her mind ticked back to all of their times together, but much to her dismay, she realized she had always been the instigator.

Her cheeks flooded with embarrassment. It was so obvious, thinking back. Her first instinct had been right; he was just a really nice guy doing her a favor. He'd played along with her to fool her parents, that was all. No matter how much she wanted him to be in love with her, the proof was in her hand. Peter was not in love with her. He was in love with Ashleigh.

That was equally mind boggling—

Peter is actually going to marry Ashleigh. That just can't be. They are so wrong for each other. But I guess it just shows I really don't know anything about love.

She groaned out loud in the dark store. The store that she now owned, thanks, in part, to Peter. The irony of it was not lost on her, and though a part of her was angry, she knew better.

Peter hadn't led her on, hadn't done anything but be a friend when she needed one. He couldn't help that she had fallen in love with him, anymore than she could help that he was marrying Ashleigh. He was just a sincerely nice man. *Who just happens to be everything I ever wanted in a man, even though I never knew I wanted one. And who is marrying someone else.*

Alex's stomach turned as she pictured the uncomfortable scene that could have played out tonight. Her declaring her love for him, and him—what would Peter have done?

The right thing, of course; kindly told her he was flattered by her feelings, or something equally as mortifying.

Then owning the store wouldn't have mattered, because I would have packed up and moved far away, left Claire to plan their wedding.

"Aghhh!" she called out into the darkness of her shop. "This could only happen to me!"

The only thing worse that she could imagine would be for him to find out. She checked her watch; he was due any minute to pick her up. No matter what, she had to convince him she only wanted to tell him she had managed to raise the money she needed and that she had let her dad know. She glanced at the fax again. If she was a big enough person, she'd congratulate him on his engagement, but she wasn't that big of a person.

That's probably his news. After all, to him, we're just friends. Why wouldn't he tell me?

The thought made the back of her throat tighten and her eyes fill. It would be more then she could take. She just had to thank him quickly for his help and get him out of the store before he had a chance to share his news with her.

A tap at the door snapped her out of her trance. Peter smiled at her through the locked door, and Alex felt a pull at her heart as she set the fax on her desk and walked to let him in.

Darn, perfect smile.

She ran her hand through her hair. This morning, she had pulled it back to the nape of her neck in a clip. Now, she could feel her unruly curls escaping here and there, one in particular at her right temple. She tried to tuck it into place as she reached the front door. Then, she took a breath, gave him a halfhearted smile, and turned the lock. Peter stepped in, his cheeks pink from the crisp night air.

"It really cooled off," Alex said absently, trying to get hold of her emotions.

Peter looked at her strangely. "It was a pretty nice day earlier. How was yours?"

Perfect, until about ten minutes ago.

"Good, lots of business." It was all she could muster. "Yours?"

"Mine, actually was better than I thought it was

going to be. You sure you're all right? You seem a little off."

Off, that was one way to describe how she felt. "Thrown off completely" was better. She wanted to tell him everything. How she had fallen madly in love with him, and if he'd just open his eyes he would see they were a perfect match. However, she wasn't up for the humiliation.

"I'm good, great, really. Never been better." She tried to sound sincere, but the effect was more of a squeak.

"Thanks for your concern, though," she added, trying to regain control.

"You're welcome," he replied, his eyes looking so deeply into hers that she shivered. "Sorry, I must have brought the cold air in with me." He placed his hand on her arm and rubbed it to try and warm her, but she only shivered again.

"No, I'm just chilled," she uttered, not able to hold his gaze anymore.

"You're not coming down with something, are you? Your cheeks are a little flushed." He put his cool hand on her forehead and Alex felt her pulse quicken. She had to get this over with or she was going to lose it.

Why does he have to be so perfect?

"Yeah, maybe. Listen, Peter, the reason I wanted to talk to you tonight was to say thank you and let you know that I got the money, and I bought the building. So we're all done." She smiled as brightly at him as she could.

A look of confusion crossed his face. "The big order came through, then? That's great, but what do you mean, 'done'?"

The mention of the big order, *his* order, brought the tightness back to Alex's throat.

"I mean, you don't have to pretend to be my boyfriend anymore. You're off the hook from my crazy family. You can get back to your life, medicine, the hospital, and whatever else." She dared to look him in the face again, and was surprised to see disappointment.

"My life?" he said absently.

"Yes. Thanks, you know, for everything. Now that you mention it, I really don't feel very well. You should probably get going in case I'm contagious or something." She rambled on, wanting the whole scene just to be over and done.

"You want me to go? What about what you needed to tell me? You know, from the other morning on the phone?"

In all the emotion, Alex had forgotten about the phone call, when she had all but told him how she felt about him.

"Um, yeah, ah, I just wanted to apologize, you know, for anything I might have done or said that was out of line that night. I really don't want to talk about it anymore. It's embarrassing. Just, I'm sorry." She looked past him to the street, and then to the display beside him, anywhere but at his intent stare.

"Seriously, you should go." She coughed a little to play up the sick thing.

God, why doesn't he just leave? This is torture.

"Oh, okay, well. I suppose I should, if that's what you want." He looked at her as if he wanted to say something else.

Alex put her hand on his arm and steered him toward the door. He didn't resist, and for that, she was grateful. They reached the door and he turned to face her.

"Alex, are you sure there's nothing else you want to tell me?"

"Just thank you, from the bottom of my heart. This store is my whole life and if I'd lost it, I don't know what I would have done. Now because of you, I don't have to find out. Thank you, Peter, for all you've done. Now go on, and don't give me a second thought. I've taken up enough of your time." There was a hint of desperation in her voice that she prayed he would take for sincerity.

Peter shook his head in disbelief, and then kissed her on the forehead. He seemed unsure what to do, so he turned and walked to the door.

But before he opened it, he turned. "Alex, there's something I have to tell you." The look of confusion had been replaced with one of determination, and Alex's heart stopped as she braced herself for his happy news.

A shrill ring split the air before Peter could continue. He reached into his pocket and pulled out his cell phone. He looked at the display and saw that it was the ER calling.

"I'm sorry, I have to take this," he apologized, surprised by how serious he now sounded.

"Dr. Gibson," he said into the phone.

"We're getting swamped here, and just got word of a big pile-up on the expressway. We need you back here immediately."

The timing couldn't be worse, but Dr. Rogers's warning rang in his ear. One slip-up and he'd be out on his ear. He had no other choice. "I'll be right there."

Peter snapped the phone closed and looked at Alex. His heart, broken from her dismissal, pounded in his chest.

"I have to get back to the hospital, but I want to finish this." He looked into her eyes. "I'll call you." Then he turned and walked out the door.

Peter walked toward the train, unsure what had just happened. Tonight was supposed to be the night he told her the truth about Ashleigh, and then declared his love for her. Now, not ten minutes after he walked into Correspondence, he was back on the street walking alone to the train. Hospital aside, she had been pushing him out before his phone rang. Had he been wrong about Alex?

He was so sure about his feelings for her. Maybe he had just convinced himself that she felt the same way. After all, she'd told him on their first date that she didn't believe in love. He must have been wrong to think he had changed her mind. The knowledge pulled at his heart as he pictured her tonight, her pink cheeks framed by the wisps of her hair, her green eyes shining.

He was sure she was falling in love with him, too, but then again, what did he know about women? Ashleigh had been his first real relationship, and look where that had gotten him. But Alex had been so different, so perfect.

It was all he could do to stop himself from going back to the store and demanding to know what was going on. But she had been in such a rush to get rid of him. Maybe she sensed that he was going to declare his love and wanted to save him the embarrassment.

That fit with Alex—she probably wouldn't know what to do with a declaration of love she didn't return.

He sighed; none of it made any sense to him. But he

didn't have time to figure it out. He had to get back to work, to the job he still had, against all odds. For tonight, he'd leave her alone, even though her dismissal hurt more than anything. When he was through with the emergency at the hospital, he'd get to the bottom of it.

The breeze from the open door rustled the cards on the front display. Alex closed the door and locked it behind him. She felt as though her heart had walked right out with him.

Sadness crept over her. She paused to straighten the cards on the wall. Alone again, and this time she actually did mind. Thoughts of Saturday nights with ice cream didn't seem nearly as appealing as they had just a few short months ago.

She couldn't even fall back on her general dislike of men, because Peter had been wonderful. It had been all her. As heartbreaking as it was to realize she wasn't going to get a happily-ever-after with him—something she didn't even believe in before meeting Peter—Alex had to admit it had felt good to believe that happily-ever-after could have actually happened for her.

Chapter Twenty-eight

Alex paused outside the restaurant and straightened her little black dress. A seafood restaurant. She couldn't believe Stephen and Claire had picked a seafood restaurant. Maybe they didn't see the irony in it. The last time she had been in the vicinity of seafood, she had ended up wearing it.

She tried not to think about what else had happened the night she had worn this dress or these heels last. When she pulled it from her closet, she was almost surprised to find that it didn't smell like shrimp at all. Not that it should; it had been dry-cleaned. To Alex, though, that night remained vivid in her mind.

In the last two months, she had thrown herself into her shop. Back to the life she had before the threat of losing her business—and before the appearance of Peter.

Claire kept after her all the time to talk about her feelings, but Alex was adamant that she had no desire to talk about what had happened. It was just too hard.

"It's not that I don't believe in love; I do. I believe in

love, just not for me. I have poor judgment in that department. Can we just leave it at that?" she said once in an attempt to quiet her friend.

Claire just gave her a look of understanding that was almost worse then rehashing the whole thing. At least she hadn't hugged her, which she had taken to doing lately. Alex hated being the object of pity.

Susan Sanders had taken the news of her "breakup" with Peter well enough. Mostly because Alex's spring line of wedding and party invitations were the "must-have" of the club set. Susan basked in her newfound celebrity status, and Alex did her best to try to bask in her mother's approval.

Alex stood waiting for her friends, feeling melancholy and reminiscent about the last few months. It was all some sort of learning experience, she was sure. And, if she didn't think specifically about the Peter part of it, it wasn't that bad.

The air was damp and full with the smell of rain, a perfect spring evening. A gust of warm wind blew her perfectly done hair out of its clip, to her irritation. She checked her watch. Seven-fifteen.

Where are Claire and Stephen? This was their idea, and now here I am, all dressed up and waiting for them.

They were going out to dinner to celebrate Stephen and Claire's engagement and the huge success of the shop. It had been Claire's idea, something out of the ordinary. She hadn't had the heart to say no to a beaming Claire, who was finally going to be a bride.

Claire and Stephen reminded Alex of how great love could be when you were lucky enough to find the right partner. They were a perfect example every time they were together. Nevertheless, Alex was a little sick of being the third wheel—the pity project.

Sure enough, the rain began—slowly and gently, but rain nonetheless. Knowing the further damage it would do to her hair, Alex hurried inside.

"By any chance have you seated a couple waiting for an Alex Sanders?" she asked the maitre d', an older man with a suspiciously thin moustache.

"No, but I have a note here for an Alex Sanders. Would you be she?"

Alex rolled her eyes, *master of the obvious.*

As hard as it was not to reply sarcastically, she bit her tongue. Instead, she just smiled and nodded. He smiled back and handed her a very thick cream envelope.

Confused, she slid her finger beneath the flap and gently opened it. The card was from Correspondence. What was Claire up to?

The front said simply: *I waited my whole life to find you.*

She flipped it open and laughed as she read the conclusion: *So, what the hell do you think is wrong with me?*

Then, written at the bottom in familiar messy penmanship:

"I've tried to forget you, but I can't. Please, just give me a chance to explain. The maitre d' can show you to my table, or you can walk out and I'll never try again. Fondly, Peter."

Alex felt her eyes fill up. Peter had called a few times, but she had always made Claire talk to him. Mrs. Rogers had sent a note saying there would be a delay in the wedding, scheduling problems or something, but Ashleigh had her heart set on the invitations for her wedding. No matter how far away that might be. Correspondence could keep their deposit.

Alex had shaken her head at the very rich and their disposable income. However, that check had been her down payment and for that, she would always be grateful to Peter, and, she supposed, to Ashleigh.

What could Peter want to explain? Her heart leapt at the thought of it, but her imagination was prone to jumping to conclusions. She should just walk out—the thought of facing his kind explanation of his love for Ashleigh would be too much to bear—but she found she couldn't.

All dressed up and now apparently set up by Claire and Stephen, Alex had no other choice.

"I believe you can show me to my table," she said to the maitre d'. He nodded, and a waiter appeared out of nowhere to lead her to a table at the back of the restaurant.

Peter sat facing her, in a shirt the blue of his eyes. His mouth curled into a tentative smile as he saw her approach, and her heart skipped a beat.

She sat. "It's good to see you, Peter," was all she could manage, her heart was racing so fast.

"More than good to see you. I didn't know if you would stay."

"And face Claire tomorrow?" Alex looked around the room, "She set this up, didn't she? Where is she?" The two of them fell into easy laughter.

"She's using hidden cameras, I think." He laughed, and Alex could feel herself calm down in his presence.

Peter reached across the table and took her hands in his and before she could pull them away, he spoke.

"Alex, that last night when I came to see you, I wanted to tell you something, but I never got the chance." He paused and looked away briefly before leaning in to continue.

"When I met you, I was involved with a girl named Ashleigh, who, I recently learned from Claire, was planning our wedding while *I* was falling in love with *you*."

Alex inhaled sharply. "But I got the fax, with your name on it as the groom. Her mother told me the wedding was still on, she wants the invitations . . ." she blurted out, not sure what to do next, but Peter squeezed her hands.

"I broke up with her the night before I saw you last. It was never that kind of relationship for me. And that was reinforced when I found out she was planning our wedding, though we were never engaged. She and I never clicked, and I didn't know why, until I met you. Then I realized—it was because I was meant to love you."

Alex's eyes filled with tears because it was how she felt, too. For the last few months, she had comforted herself with the thought that she had loved Peter—even if she couldn't be with him. Now, he was saying exactly what she had dreamed of hearing.

She looked across the table to see tears in his eyes, too.

"I was meant to love you, too," she said. Then, overcome with need for him, she stood to kiss him.

Somehow, in her haste, her heels tangled in the tablecloth, and a familiar sense of déjà vu set in as she tried to recover her balance—to no avail.

As she wavered, Peter jumped out of his chair, catching her as she fell. He pulled her close, his arms gripping her tightly, their faces inches apart.

"I'll do my best not to let you fall again," he whispered, his eyes meeting hers as he leaned in to kiss her.

Alex pulled away and looked into his eyes. Her pulse quickened. "Even if I fall for you?" Peter smiled that perfect smile, and she continued. "Then, I'm afraid, you're too late." She laughed at the absolute cheesiness of the line.

But heck, maybe that's what love does to a sensible girl.

Then she kissed him again, her heart pounding, but her feet planted firmly on the floor.